I Am Also A Human

Jasbir Singh

Invincible Publisher

First published in India in 2018

ISBN: 978-93-87328-55-6

Invincible Publishers

G-120, Sushant Lok III, Sector 57, Gurgaon-122002

Registered Address: Opposite Kasturba Ashram, Radaur, Haryana - 135133

Printed at Thomson Press (India) LTD

For all the people who belong to the third gender community.
A small salute for their sacrifices and struggles.

For Papa, your words always motivate me in life.

Acknowledgement

There are certain people who play an important role in one's life. When I wrote this book, yes, I did the actual writing, but if certain people wouldn't have been with me during this writing journey, then the whole writing process would become exponentially difficult! I would like to thank these people for being there to help me and understand my ideas when I was writing this book.

A trillion times, thanks to God for his love, blessings, and showing me the right path.

My family- for freeing me from my daily chores and letting me work in peace. Papa, you left me three years ago, but you are always in my heart, your words keep motivating me. Maa, for serving my meals next to my laptop, on my table, three times a day and taking the plates back. Gurdeep Kaur, for always being so caring. Why are elder sisters so caring?

My friends, who make my life priceless. I have not told you yet, friends, but believe me, without your love and support, I am nothing. You are my biggest strength. It is strange but this is one of the reasons I am with you. Thank you so much, guys, for being so real with me. Thank you for being in my life and supporting me in all ups and downs of my life. Guys, you are the real gems of my life.

Let me now, thank the people who are very special to me.

Simran thanks for being with me in all phases of my life.

My special thanks to my first reader, sister, and a very good friend Manya Sharma. A big thanks to you for giving me feedback every time, caring like a sister, and supporting me like a best friend. Aradhna Sharma and Sadhna Sharma, our friendship is about six years old. Thanks for motivating me everytime and letting me know that I can write. Khushbu Verma, I met you few months ago and you're an amazing person. Thanks for motivating me every time.

Thanks to those friends who helped me at various stages and encouraged me to do better and to write better— Suyash Gupta, Apurv Gupta, Mrinal Jha, Ekjot Kaur, Jagdeep Singh, Jitendra Kumar, Asfaque Hussain, Neetu Bhatiya, Eknoor Deep, and Sonia Sharma.

Teachers play an important role in your life. My school time teacher, Dr.Atul Hans, Sir, you're my role model. Preet Kanwal ma'am, Kiran Thakur ma'am, Adnan Sidqui sir, and Dr. Pawan Kumar sir- thanks for sharing your knowledge with me and making me a better human.

I don't have a long friends' list on Facebook. But, to all my Facebook friends, thank you for trusting me without even reading a single page of my manuscript. A few of you have been more than amazing— Harman Kaur, Smily Verma, your words are decidedly profound. You both are amazing writers. Susmita Adhikari, Dilshad Ansari, Srisha Adhikary, and Deepa Karki- Your love and support from Nepal encourages me to write better. I really love you all.

A big thanks to the entire team at Invincible Publishers.

Mirnal Jha, Asfaque Hussain, and Ankush Kumar thanks for making the video in a very short period.

Mrinal Jha, you are more than a brother. You keep supporting me in all my endeavors.

Asfaque Hussain, bro, you're a great artist. You click smiles not photos. Your photos are amazing. Thanks for everything.

Manish Raj, you are like a big brother. A big thanks to you for handling all the marketing.

Special thanks to Lovely Professional University for supporting and giving me such a wonderful and enriching environment.

In the end, I thank myself for travelling to different cities to find stories for this book. For keeping a spirit of never giving up and writing with my heart. When I had started writing this book, I did not think I would be able to complete it, but I am happy that I finally made it.

This is an inspirational and romantic tale that starts with Zeenat, our protagonist. This story highlights social issues that have become a part of our society. It is an inspirational tale of a person who is trying to say only one thing i.e. "I AM ALSO A HUMAN." Treat me as you would treat other people treated in the society.

Welcome to the inspirational journey of Zeenat: a story that has a mix of love, sacrifice, suspense, feelings, and highlights the hypocrisy of our society.

About the Author

Jasbir Singh is a contemporary Indian author. He was born on 12 November 1997 in the state of Jammu & Kashmir in India. He is pursuing a degree in Bachelor of Business Administration from Lovely Professional University.

He devotes most of his time to social work. He is the former founder of Youth Foundation (an NGO). Presently, he is the founder of an NGO named Vigilante in Kathmandu, Nepal. He wrote his first novel 'Forever: A Promise' at the age of nineteen. This is his second novel which is inspired by social issues.

At present, he lives in Jalandhar, Punjab. He likes to travel and cook. He wants to bring some change in the society and to inspire people with his words. He likes to sit alone and analyze the people's behavior. He also writes cooking recipes. He is quite social and believes in the words, "Live for others; live for others' happiness."

For updates from him and to know him more, follow him:
On Facebook page: www.facebook.com/writerjasbirsingh
On Instagram: jasbir_rissam
On Twitter: @jasbirsingh1233
On Website: www.jasbirsingh.net

I am also a human, I have the right to live,
I have feelings, I have the right to feel,
I am transgender, I never feel ashamed for my identity,
For I am the first and long last,
I belong to this world, I have the right to love,
Doesn't matter if I cannot give birth to child,
But I can adopt a child, I am the mother
I am the sister and friend,
I am the beloved,
I can become someone's inspiration,
I am the wife of my husband,
I am also a human, I have the right to live.
I did so many things which are shameful for society,
Many times, I harassed for my gender,
Many times, I insulted for my gender,
But still I'm living in this world,
Because every time it made me strong,
I am also a human, I have the right to live.
I do have also dreams, for my lover,
I also want to spend my rest of life, without any tension,
harassment,
I'm waiting for those days,
I'm waiting for my lover,
Always respect me for my every work, for I am the shameful
and magnificent one,
I am a transgender,
But I am also a human, I have the right to live.

Prologue

We are children of mother India. There is so much diversity in our country. People from different states, different religions, different languages, different food habits and so many other things live together. Everyone has the right and freedom to live in their own way. After all, it is the most democratic country in the world. However, have you ever given a thought about those people who are made to think that they are not even human?

Have you thought about those who, without any mistake of their own, living a life no better thanliving in hell on Earth?

We are all humans. All of us have emotions, feelings and the right to do the thing we like, do what we want. But does this right apply to everyone? Anyone who takes birth on this Earth is a creature of God, and nobody has the right to say anything to them.

By reading these words, you may wonder what the author really wants to convey.

What do you know about the people who belong to the transgender community?

I want to put this one question out to all the people of the world.

Are the people who identify as transgender or third gender really impure? Do they not have the right to live in this world? Oh, maybe 'World' is too vast; have they no right to live in this society?

I hate labels, especially when talking about minorities (the third gender). They are just normal people. They eat the same food, breathe the same air, walk in the same manner, take birth from their mother the same way as us, and sleep just like us all.

They aren't some aliens from another planet! They are humans.

They might look scary or maybe they appear too overwhelming in their makeup, but behind all that facade, there is a human being, an innocent person who is seeking love, who is trying to fit into the society, desperate to live a dignified life, be loved by someone and be happy. But our society treats them as if they belong to some other planet.

Don't **HARASS** them for their gender,

Don't **HATE** them for their identity,

Love them, because they are beautiful creatures of God,

Love them, because they are also HUMAN.

What gender do words define?

According to me, there are three genders: male, female, and transgender. Our government has done great work by giving them their rights in our society. Still, there are many social rights for which they are fighting for every day.

The issue of gender is so important in our society, yet it has filled so much negativity in the minds of the people.

Okay...

Let's travel by this novel and meet some interesting people, learn about their stories of courage, sacrifice, and love.

Of the many characters in the novel, the name of our protagonist is Zeenat.

Zeenat: A beautiful girl. Here, we are not talking about outer beauty; she is beautiful by heart. In her society, everyone loves her, but she has so many things to say. She is also a transgender

•••

Rajveer: A dashing, handsome, and rich guy from Delhi. He has everything in his life. He is a stud and famous among girls. He has multiple girlfriends at any particular time.

Ram: A social worker. He is also good by heart. He helps the needy.

Shanaya: A rich, egoistic girl. She has an ego because her father is rich. She wants everything in life; by hook or by crook. Oh! she is also Rajveer's childhood friend.

Rahul: A rich guy. Best friend to Rajveer and Shanaya. He is also very egoistic. Both Rahul and Shanaya hate poor people, as they feel poor people have no right to live in the society.

Are they right? Are they going to commit a huge mistake which might change everyone's life?

What will happen when all of them meet at one place and a new phase of their life begins?

What happens when life makes a 'Square of Love' in their life?

These characters will show you the true face of the society and our behavior towards the transgenders.

A Nightmare

Once upon a time, there lived a Zeenat. Before I go on, let me tell you that she belongs to the transgender community. Now let's start from the very beginning.

Hey, I'm Zeenat. One day, you will read about me but at that time I might not be alive. I actually want to commit suicide. Well, I'm a prostitute from last five years. I still remember the day I was raped. Hope vanished from my life five years ago. However, something has been bothering me for the last few days. Whenever I see him, I feel like his eyes are saying something to me. But now, these things don't matter to me. Every day, he pays money to the broker, just like the other people, and comes to my room. The weird thing is, he has not touched me yet. While I like that about him, it is a little strange because people come here just to fulfill their sexual needs.

The area where I have been living for the last five years, the red-light district of Delhi known by the name of 'GB Road', is the worst place in all of India according to the society.

I don't know why, but initially, he used to visit two or three times a week. Each time he would choose me. Then he started to visit every day. Days flew by and his visits didn't stop. I thought I should ask him the reason for this weird behavior.

That day, like every other day, he came, sat on a chair, picked up a magazine and started reading it. But I wanted answers to my questions, so, I started removing my clothes because here people come just to fuck you, not caring for your physical or mental state. After living in this type of area, you can't expect anything from anyone because nobody cares for you. They come just to fulfill their sexual desires because this is what they are paying for. It so happens that money can also buy people respect; as here people sell their respect for money, either forcefully or with consent.

He looked up and his eyes opened wide in shock. As he stood up, he raised his hands as he almost shouted, “Stop! Stop! Stop this nonsense! What are you doing?”

“I'm just removing my clothes. You have paid to fuck me then just do it. That is what people come here for; I have been raped by 108 people till now. How can I expect you to be any different?”

“What are you saying? Please, don't say such things, I don't need anything from you.”

“So what do you want from me? Earlier, you used to come here two or three times a week, now you come daily. Your pay a lot of money just to spend time with me why?

“Right now, I cannot answer your question. You just need to trust me, I can help you get out from this place.”

"Do I look like a fool to you? My feelings and emotions died a few years ago, now I am a mere shell of a body without a soul."

“I know these people bring thousands of girls each year from different parts of the country and from Nepal. They force them to work here and even send a few girls to other parts of the world. I know you have tried to unsuccessfully run away five times in the last few years. I know you want to leave. I know how they treat you. I know some of these girls are working consensually. But there are others like you who are forced to be here. Help me help you. At least think about the other girls as well!”

“How do you know so much about this place and me? Who are you? What do you want from me? See, I cannot help you. I'm happy with this place now as I no longer have any hopes or expectations from life. I just want to die. I have tried committing suicide too, but I failed. I hate seeing myself in this condition. Do you have any idea how we live here? There are times when we have more than 10 customers coming into our room in a single day and we have to fulfill their sexual needs and demands as per their payment. We just have to lay on the bed and they start having sex with us in a brutal manner. They don't care about us. They just want to fulfill their sexual desires. Something dies within me each time they touch my body and sleep with me."

"I know I cannot feel the pain you have been going through for past five years, but I can help you to escape. I run an NGO that works for those who are forced to work here. We have helped many girls and now they are living their life happily, you can also become one of them if you want."

"We have faced so many things here and my trust has been broken far too many times. I cannot trust anyone anymore."

"You have to trust me. Every girl here respects you and has faith in you. You need to do something for them and give them a happy future. I will help you in this; I will stand by your side no matter what the situation."

"Please give me some time. I will have to think about all this."

"Zeenat, Zeenat, Zeenat open the door," Begum Jaan shouted.

"Coming, Begum Jaan." The moment I opened the door, she pushed me and entered the room. Ram was lying on the bed.

"These days you are spending so much time with Zeenat. Is everything alright?" Begum Jaan enquired, looking at Ram.

"Yes, Begum Jaan everything is good. Don't worry," he replied with a coy smile.

"Is she fulfilling your needs or not?"

"Absolutely Begum Jaan she is very good at her work. She is fulfilling all my needs. That's why I come here repeatedly."

Convinced with Ram's replies, Begum Jaan left the room.

"I assure you that from now on I'll support you in each and every step of your life. So, don't worry," Ram touched my hand reassuringly as he said this.

"Ok, but I need some time to take a decision."

"It's ok; I'll wait for your reply. Bye, take care!"

He came towards me and hugged me softly. The moment he hugged me, I felt different. I felt like Rajveer was hugging me but I knew that was impossible. He left the room.

From past many days, he was the only customer who chose me. In this profession, people prefer young girls and I have been working here for five years now. People don't want females who are28 years and above. The fact that I am a transgender adds to the reasons why I am not the chosen one.

I had no regrets; instead, I was happy as I was with Ram. He wanted to help us and after a really long time, I felt safe in someone's presence.

A sudden realization hit me that a transgender has no life despite where they live, be it in society with people or in such a place which is called 'cheap'. So, I just sat in my room as I knew that nobody will come.

I contemplated Ram's words, but I was in a dilemma whether to trust him or not. Will he really help us? I finally went to bed and kept thinking about it the whole night.

The next morning, I had decided that I would help him. Now, I just had to wait for him to plan things further.

I knew he would come this Friday as he had mentioned he would be free that day. Till then I just had to hide from Begum Jaan because if she comes to know that I'm free these days, she will definitely send some customers to my room.

I heard Begum Jaan shouting my name.

"Zeenat, Zeenat, Zeenat, Where are you?"

"I'm in my room, Begum Jaan," I replied.

She entered my room and I was scared thinking that she may have sent a new customer. I realized I wanted to spend time with Ram, no one else, I didn't want to entertain any other customer. I was getting a bit selfish but I felt comfortable and happy with Ram. I spent my days remembering him. I knew that what I was doing was wrong, but my senses were not under my control. Finally, the day came when he paid Begum Jaan and entered my room. I started crying the moment I saw him and hugged him tightly. I didn't know why I hugged him, all I knew was that I had longed for this hug for a really long time.

I cried for more than three hours and he made every possible effort to make me happy which was most beautiful. He took my hand in his hands and asked, "What happened, Zeenat?"

"Nothing, it's just that I'm a very emotional person and have seen a lot of things in life, but after a really long time I feel that there is someone who is supporting me and I feel safe around you."

"I have been waiting to hear these words for so long! I am happy that you have finally realized how much I care for you. Thank you very much."

"Sometimes, we realize few things very late, but when we do, we give our best to hold on."

"Yeah, you are totally right. I have discussed the complete scenario with my team and the local police as well. We decided that this Monday, my team and local police will raid this place at an hour when all the girls will be working. Would that work?"

“Yes! The plan is good but please make sure that everything goes smoothly and no one is hurt.”

“Sure. Don't worry. I can do anything to make you happy. You are my motivation. I don't care what other people say, I don't care what other people think. For me your smile is everything. You are an Angel because you brighten up my life. That's why I promised that I'll stand by you at all times. Now, you are the reason that I am alive.”

After saying these words, he cuddled with me, kissed my forehead and said, "Don't worry. Everything will be good. Trust me.”

The moment he kissed my forehead, I felt his love for me. I was also falling for him because of his care, love, and respect towards me. All girls want such a person in her life who loves her, respects her, gives her value in life, trusts her, and always stands by her in every situation of life. I knew he was the right person for me. Now, I was waiting for Monday when I'll leave with him for good.

Days went by fast. Everyday customers kept coming and the girls kept doing their jobs perfectly. When I tried running away from here and got caught each time, I had resigned to the fact that this is my life. I have to live here and sell my body forever. I felt like I had been born only to fulfill sexual needs of others, but now things were changing. I had started dreaming of a happy life.

Finally, Monday arrived and just like every other day I was getting ready. I was happy. I couldn't tell this to anyone but I knew that soon some girls will get the chance to live happily. I was waiting for him in my room.

“Zeenat, Zeenat, Zeenat.”

Begum Jaan was shouting my name.

“Come down. Someone is waiting for you,” she called.

The moment I heard these words, I started running but then I saw a man in his sixties standing near Begum Jaan.

"Come here, Zeenat," she said.

"Zeenat, today you are looking very beautiful. Listen, this is your new customer. Today you have to entertain him the same way you entertain Ram so he also becomes a regular customer."

"No, Begum Jaan, I can't do it. Besides Ram will becoming today. He will be disappointed at not being with me. You don't want to lose a regular customer, do you?" I tried pleading.

"Zeenat, either you entertain him on your own or else I will have to force you."

"No, I can't do this. I told you I am waiting for Ram, he will even pay more!"

"Naresh, Ajay, come here. Take her to her room. I will have to teach her again today."

They dragged me by my arms to my room and the man followed them. They started tying my hands and legs. I shouted for help but nobody was there to rescue me.

They tied me and left the room but the man was standing right in front of my eyes. I wanted to kill him before he touches me but I was helpless.

He started removing his clothes. I closed my eyes. As the sound of his feet increased in volume, I could sense that he was coming closer. I started shivering and could not stop my tears. I had been raped by 108 people but this time the situation was different because my heart and body now belonged to Ram.

He came closer and started touching my body and removing my clothes. He was touching my private parts and I couldn't stop crying.

• • •

Suddenly Ram entered the room and slapped the man. The policemen ran to other rooms and caught others too. Ram rushed towards me, untied me and gave me a warm, reassuring hug.

"I have promised to stand by you at all times, haven't I? Now, forget everything and let's start a new life," Ram said as he wiped my tears.

"Sure. I always wanted to start a new life but I lost all hopes until you came and changed everything. Thank you for everything."

He kept his promise and he and his team helped the other girls to get a happy life again. I was very happy with his work as I always wanted to help the needy people. He also made arrangements to send the other girls to habilitation center as they were not in a good shape.

At the moment, we were sitting in a car. A driver was driving and we kept looking at each other.

"Where are we going?" I asked.

"We are going to my house. From now on, you will be living there with me," Ram replied.

"I don't want to be a burden on your shoulders. I can handle myself. You don't need to worry; I will find a home for myself. I have already put you in a lot of trouble."

"It's nothing like that. I have promised that I'll be with you in every situation and I'm just fulfilling my promise."

"I don't want to take anymore help from you. I don't do anything for you and you are doing so much for me. It makes me feel like I am selfish."

"Don't think so much, just take a deep breath and listen to me. If you want to go, you can leave at any time. But stay with me until you find a home and a job. We are not discussing anything more on this topic."

“Ok. I'll stay at your place but I’ll leave once I find a home and some work for myself.”

“Thank you for considering my words.”

“You don’t need to thank me; you have already done so much for me. You are the most altruistic person I have ever come across.”

He smiled. His smile reminded me of all that was good in the society. It made me want to make an effort to help the needy and make the world a better place.

Finally, after much chit-chat we reached his house. It was situated in the Kabootar Chowk of Connaught Place, Delhi. I opened the gate and we entered the house. It was beautiful.

"This is my bedroom, this is the lobby, this is the kitchen, and this is your room. How's it?" Ram showed me around the house.

"A person who comes from a place where she sold her body now comes to a house like this, this can only be a dream. Obviously, I love it."

“I'm glad that you like it because only a few people like my place.”

“Indeed, I like it very much.”

“Do you know how to cook butter chicken?” he asked.

“Yeah, I know but why are you asking me this?”

“I love butter chicken. I'm a big foodie. So, from now on you will cook tasty food for me. This will be your duty.”

“Sure! Well, cooking is my hobby. I love to cook different cuisines.”

“Ok, let's start from today. You will prepare today's dinner.”

“Ok, Fine.”

We both went to our respective rooms.

•••

I kept thinking about my earlier life, it felt like a nightmare has ended. Now, I can spend the rest of my life happily but with whom?

I don't know anyone. Everybody is new to me, a stranger for me, except for Ram.

Ram came in like God and changed my life. I spent all night thinking about the rest of my life and what I'll do further.

Next morning, I woke up at 6 a.m. and cleaned the house. I prepared breakfast for him along with black coffee which I knew was his favorite. When it was about 10 a.m., I knocked at his door, "Ram, Ram."

"Yes, what happened Zeenat? Come on in."

I entered the room and saw him lying on his bed.

"I have something for you. You have done so much for me. I owe it to you."

"What is it? And please stop saying that I have done a lot for you."

"Ok. Fine. Don't spoil your mood now. Wait, I'll be right back."

I brought him his black coffee and breakfast from the kitchen.

"Here, this is for you. Have it."

"Wow!! How did you know that I start my morning with black coffee?"

"Since you know so many things about me, it's my responsibility to know few things about you too."

"Why is it that whenever I talk to you, I feel like I'm talking to a mature person who has sacrificed a lot in life?"

"It's nothing like that…or maybe you are right."

"Zeenat, I want to know about your past, your family, your siblings, your friends, relatives, everything."

"See, in everyone's life something or the other happens which they do not want to share with anyone and same is the case with me."

“But you can share with me; I want to know each and everything about your life.”

“Why do you want to know? My story is not that special; it’s just that I have seen our society’s true face and I know that society will never accept people like us.”

“You might be right because you have faced a lot of things but slowly their mindsets are changing and they will accept you one day. You should not care about others, just live your life happily.”

“I seriously don't care about others anymore.”

"That’s great! Just remember I'll always be there for you at all points in your life from now on. So, you don't need to worry at all."

“I trust you and I know you will never break my trust.”

“Thank you for trusting me.”

“I have to freshen up now as I'm getting late for office. We will talk later.”

“Sure.”

He went to the bathroom and I again started thinking about myself and what I will do now. I realized that since my dream has always been to help the needy people, I could join Ram in his NGO and work for the welfare of the people. He could guide me as he has so much experience in this field. There is a chance for me to work with him.

He came out of his room and was shocked to see everything so clean.

“Where are you Zeenat?”

I came from the kitchen, “What happened?”

"Did you clean my house? There was no need of this but seriously the house looks beautiful now."

"Hahaha... nothing like that. I just woke up early and thought to clean the house."

"Okay. Good. Oh!! I'm getting late. Bye, I'm going."

"Bye."

I watched television the whole day. Ram told me not to go to market alone but I was getting bored so I decided to go for vegetable shopping as I needed to buy mushrooms for dinner. They were Ram's favorite. As I was roaming in the market, I heard a voice, "How much will you charge for tonight? 200, 500, or 1000?"

As soon as I heard those words I started running because I realized that they recognized me. Finally reached home. I was thought that I left my past there but I forgot that people do not forget. They will always remember me as Zeenat, the one who worked on GB road. I have nothing left. I should leave this world.

As I was thinking all this, the doorbell rang. I opened the door, it was Ram.

"What happened, Zeenat?"

"Nothing."

"Something has happened. Look at your eyes. These eyes are telling me a lot."

"Don't be a fool. Nothing has happened."

"Ok, fine."

"Actually, today in the evening I went to the vegetable market there some people recognized me and started asking how much I will take for tonight. I realized that this is my identity and it will never leave me."

“It is not like that. Please don't care about others. They will call you these things but you have to learn to ignore them. You have a chance to start a new life. Don't leave this because of some people. Fulfill your dreams, do something for the society. Isn’t that you have always wanted to do?”

“You are right. I want to do something for the society but I don't how to go about it.”

"You can work with me. You have that spark to motivate others. We need people like you on our team."

“I don't know what I would say. You have already done so much for me and now you are offering me this.”

“See, I'm not doing anything special for you. We need people like you and we will pay you according to the work you do. I am not doing anyfavour to you here.”

“Ok. Then I'll work with you.”

“Good.”

“I asked you how you ended up in a place like that in the first place, you didn't answer.”

“I don't want to remember my past with anyone.”

“Sometimes we should share our past with someone, it gives us inner peace and you really need it.”

“You want to know then listen.”

“Thank you.”

"I was harassed for my gender and was insulted for my identity. My parents sent me to an orphanage when I was just twelve. I was even raped by someone when I was sixteen. I never asked anything to anyone. I know I'm a transgender but that was not my mistake. I know I was not useful for the society. I somehow survived for twenty-eight years in this world but never complained. Five years ago, I met someone who used to bring a smile to my face whenever I felt sad. I had someone who fought with the whole world just for me. I had someone who was the reason for my smile, the reason for my living. Then suddenly, one day, I had nothing and no one with me. I lost all my patience and strength. I just wanted to die. I just wanted to say goodbye to this cruel world. I wanted to go...He was waiting for me in the afterlife, was there for me, anymore. Actually, it didn’t affect anyone because life goes on, it does not stop for anyone. People come and go; death is the bitter truth of life and I am a burden on society. Just because I am a transgender nobody cared about me. But my soul wanted to ask so many questions from this world...What was my fault?

Was this lack of care due to the face that I am a Transgender or that I dared to love someone or I thought about myself or I fought with people for harassing me or because I didn't raise a voice when I was being raped?

If this was my fault, then I'm very happy because whatever happened to me was my destiny and I accepted it.

Maybe in any other world, there is someone who can understand me that ‘I AM ALSO A HUMAN'. Someone who understand us that ‘We are also HUMANS'."

I had a Dream

Like all other girls, I was too born with an innocent smile. In my adolescence, like every other girl, I too dreamt of my prince charming and how I will meet him. I was a princess in my eyes. I dreamt of a rich, handsome, intelligent man and getting married to him, my prince, wearing a wonderful wedding dress. I know now that I cannot give birth to a child, but at the time I thought of becoming a mother and having two beautiful kids who would take care of me in my old age. We would all live in a lovely house, not a big one but a comfortable one, which would be filled with loads of happiness.

I still had dreams and it is not a crime to think and dream of a beautiful future for oneself. I forgot about my past, but I didn't know that one day my past will come and destroy all my future plans right in front of my eyes.

When I was born, my parents were not happy as they wanted a boy but destiny had something else planned. We were not rich. My father was a factory worker in Bihar and my mother worked as a housemaid for other people. My hometown was in Gaya, Bihar which had one cinema hall and only a few banks. Gaya is famous for Bodh Gaya, a religious site, and place of pilgrimage associated with the Maha bodhi temple. I had hoped that one day my prince charming would come, sweep me off my feet, and take me away with him to another place and I would have my happily ever after.

But I had no right to think about myself, I was not allowed to dream. After few years, I think, when I was twelve, my mother took me along to one of the houses where she worked.

When my mother was working and I was lying on the bed, one lady came and started playing with me. She held me in her hands and asked my mom for my name.

My mom very happily replied, “Zeenat.”

“She is my daughter, the angel of our life.”

The lady looked very happy to hear this.

"Wait, she is not a girl," the lady told my mother.

I didn't understand what she was saying at that time, but I knew whatever she said was serious.

My mom was surprised.

“What do you mean?” My mom asked.

"She is a transgender. You were expecting a boy, she is transgender." As she told these words to my mom, she threw me from her hands as if she was throwing garbage on the ground.

"You have to live your whole life with her. She will be a burden for your family; in fact, she would be a big stigma for your whole family."

“What are you saying? She is our angel. We both love her and don’t care if she is a transgender or not. She is our life. We will take care of her.”

“Well, that is very good but if you want can I give you an advice?"

“Yeah, sure tell me.”

"You can send Zeenat to an orphanage; they will take care of her. Many children who are like her live there. It would be a better place for her and whenever you feel like meeting her, you can go there and meet her. There she will get a good education and will be treated well."

That was when my mother came to know that she had given birth to a transgender. My mother felt disappointed, all her dreams vanished. She was crying about her destiny but was helpless. She never imagined a thing like this happening. After hearing all this, my mom finished her work and we headed home.

Internally my mom was upset on hearing this news but this was destiny. None of us could do anything or change this, we were helpless.

My mom reached home and told everything to my father. My whole family was disappointed and lost hope because they knew, nobody would marry a transgender. Thus, my parents decided to send me to an orphanage.

How can parents decide to send their own child to an orphanage? I was only 12 years old and had no knowledge of the society. I was like a flower that was in the initial stages of growth and wanted to spread happiness all around the world.

At that time, I was not mature enough to even understand the difference between a home and an orphanage but my destiny was something else. I could do nothing but just wait for some good days and dream of a good life.

I will never forget that black day of my life: 28th May 2004; well it would be a black day for every child whose parents were planning to send him/her to an orphanage. Nobody wants to go there, in fact, the only kids who have to go there are the unfortunate ones who have lost their parents but my situation was different as I was dead to my parents.

Sometimes, I think I was never their child because they refused to accept me as one.

It was Thursday midnight and everyone was sleeping in their respective homes. I was awake in fear, I was scared as I didn't know when I will have to leave my house and my parents will send me to the orphanage.

I just kept changing positions on the bed anxiously and started thinking about life. I was not mature at that time but I knew one thing for sure that my parents were going to do something very bad to me.

I loved my parents very much, but did they love me? To this date, I haven't found an answer to this question.

Soon it was Friday morning, the date was May 28th, 2004 and I was sleeping on my bed. My mom came to me early in the morning and tried to wake me up.

"Zeenat wake up, wake up Zeenat."

She was shouting. I had never seen her like this before; perhaps this was the first sign.

After hearing my mom shout, I finally decided to wake up.

I woke up, got fresh, and did all my morning rituals before heading for breakfast.

When I was having my breakfast, I didn't know what was going to happen to me.

I took the first bite, the taste was a bit different but I ignored that because I was very hungry. After finishing my breakfast, I was felt sleepy again. Well, this was unusual as I never felt sleepy after breakfast, it made me little suspicious but I was in no condition to think.

I chose to go to my room and sleep again.

I woke up in the evening around 6 p.m., I didn't remember the time exactly but yeah it was evening time.

A Broken Dream

As I opened my eyes, I found myself in a different place; many people were looking at me. It scared me a little because everyone was a stranger and I had no clue of what was happening with me.

After few minutes, everyone stepped back and I saw a lady, well... she didn't exactly look. like a lady. I had not seen people like her earlier. I squinted my eyes for a better look as she came towards me. She wore a lot of jewelry, a heavy sari, and had too much of makeup on her face.

Everyone was touching her feet and taking blessings. It looked like she was everyone's mother. Finally, she reached my bed and placed her hand on my head.

Most of the people were calling her "Rajiya Amma".

I later learned that her name was Rajiya or we can also say "Rajiya Amma".

"Now, you are a part of our family. No need to worry. We will love you. You are safe here," said Rajiya Amma.

I didn't understand what she was saying.

"Which place is this? Can you tell me where am I? Where are my parents? I just want to go home. I want to go. Please leave me. Allah!!! Help me!" I started shouting.

"You are in a safe place. We don't know who left you here, but from now on you are our responsibility."

"I have parents. I have my mom and dad. I want to go home. I don't want to live here. Please leave me."

She understood that my parents had left me here because of my gender. She smiled and said, "From now on, we are your parents, we are your family because your parents have left you here."

Well for some time I was in shock. What was happening with me? I realized that I have no one in my life anymore. At a very tender age, I had realized many things about life.

Rajiya Amma was talking to me continuously, but I was not in the condition to utter even a word. I silently sat on a chair and thought about my destiny. I blamed God for my condition and asked him why had he sent me on this Earth. Why was I born in such a family who don't care about their child?

At the tender age of twelve, I had endless questions but nobody could give me the answers. I kept waiting for the day when someone would come in my life and say, "Zeenat, your smile is the reason of my living, you are my motivation and you are my inspiration."

I didn't talk to anyone there. Everyone was talking about me. I saw few girls elder than me who were playing and eating happily. I think I was the youngest of the lot. I could not digest how a person could forget their families so easily. I knew my parents didn't do good with me still, somewhere in my heart I still loved and respected them.

If I ever got a chance to go home, I would happily choose my home but I knew it was never going to happen. Maybe that's the reason they were so much happy here.

I know it would take some time to adjust here but I realized that now they are my family. I have to live my whole life with them. Nobody was going to come and take me out from here.

I lost my dreams.

I lost my positive vibes.

Each day, Rajiya Amma came to me and wanted to talk to me but I remained silent. In the real sense, I just wanted to die. I didn't want to live anymore. I didn't want to talk to anyone.

She tried her best to make me happy, to bring a smile to my face. I knew that she was doing all this just for me but I had lost my smile. I didn't want to give a fake smile.

I rememberit was 14th of July when she had organized a small and beautiful event for me, just to bring a smile on my face.

I was sitting on the bench and everyone was dancing and doing different acts but I just sat with my eyes fixed on the floor.

The event came to an end. Everyone tried their best. I was feeling selfish who don't care about other people's feelings. Well, I became that type of person who was just happy with her own life because I had no hope left within me.

For the next two years, I sat alone, silently, not talking to anyone. Every day, Rajiya Amma came to me, tried talking to me. I don't know why each time, she would put in so much effort to talk to me. She always showed kindness and behaved like I was her daughter.

On 4th August 2006 finally, my heart melted and I thought I should talk to her. Well, it was for a selfish motive but I really didn't want talk to anyone else about this.

"Hello, Rajiya Amma," I called.

I didn't know that I should call her by her name or not.

She just smiled.

“Amma, I want to talk to you.”

“Yes sure, my dear daughter.” I think it was the first time that she referred someone as her daughter.

I walked towards her, everyone lived there was scared to talk to her but I was very good, I was very happy, I didn't feel scared.

I sat on the bench beside her.

She put her hands on my head and gave me a tight hug. After a long time, I felt better.

She kept looking at me. I asked, “What happened, Amma?”

She was silent. She didn't say anything.

I asked again, “Tell me, what happened?”

She smiled and said, “I was wondering that how parents can be so cruel that they leave their children in an orphanage just because of their gender.”

The moment she said this, my tears started to roll down from my eyes because I knew she was talking about me. I was unable to speak anything because I had realized earlier that nobody in this world would love you more than yourself. So, that's why I left every hope back and now I have to do something for myself.

Each moment that I spent with her, I remembered the early days of my life when I was also a normal child when people loved me and cared for me. Today, nobody loved me not even my parents.

I was started feeling sleepy and slowly my eyes closed even when I was still in her arms. The next morning, she came to my room.

“How are you feeling now?” she asked.

“I'm feeling good.”

I had realized that I have to change my behavior towards them and gel with them.

"You have done so much for me just to put a smile on my face. Everyone here respects you. I neither gave you any respect nor responded to you still you kept trying. Why?"

“Daughter, sometimes we do something selflessly and I do not have an answer to your questions.”

“I know and sometimes this makes me realize that we still have so much to do. Life does not end here. Now I will do everything for myself and will not care about others.”

“That’s good, but always remember one thing, never forget the ones who help you in your hard days. Always remember them and return the favour.”

“Yes sure.”

“I have planned something for you, my dear, and it will help you in the future.”

“Ok, what is it?”

“I'll tell you everything but only when the right time comes. Well, be prepared tomorrow and soon your studies will start.”

“Studies?”

"Yes, studies. I want that you to study and work in a good place. I want to make you an independent person and you must live your life like other people. You are very special to me and I want you to become a good person who can help others and live a respectful life."

“From this day onwards, you are my mom and dad and I'll do everything and make you feel proud.”

“I knew that one day you would realize the bitter truth of the society and I'm very happy that you realized this at such an early age. This will make you stronger.”

“Yes, life has taught me a lot of things.”

“Amma, Amma,” Dheeraj was calling her.

Dheeraj was quite close to Rajiyaamma. He was also the caretaker. Whenever she went outside, he took care of everything. He was about 27 years old and had just returned from a journey.

He came and touched her feet.

“How was your journey, Dheeraj?”

“Amma, it was good. I enjoyed a lot.”

“Good. Now, go and take some rest.”

"Yes, amma but before that, I want to visit the ashram. May I go?"

“You just returned from a long journey and you want to visit the ashram. No, first go and take some rest.”

“Please, amma, please.”

“Ok fine go.”

“Thank you, amma. I love you.”

He hugged her and left the place.

"He is a very good person. We all love him. Like you, he has nobody in his life. His parents had left him here. He has spent twenty-six years here. Now, he is educated and wants to do something for us. He has so many ideas and plans and I want the same thing for you. He will teach you everything. He will teach you the lessons of life."

I was sixteen and was studying in ashram from last four years but I didn't understand what studies she was talking about. Since that was what Amma wanted, I said yes to her.

So, from tomorrow he will be teaching me but when I saw him the next day I got a strange feeling.

• • •

Broken Soul

It was around 7:30 a.m. and I was lying on the bed with my eyes half-closed. I heard some voices like someone was coming towards my room. After a few minutes, someone knocked on my door. I remember that winter day of 21st January 2007, when for the first time I felt unsafe in this place. I did not feel like opening the door but the knocking was continuous. A hoarse male voice came in:

"Zeenat, Zeenat."

"Please go from here, I want to sleep for some more time."

"No, your classes will start at 8 a.m. and you are still sleeping. Wake up now."

"No, I will wake up when I want, so you just go from here. Don't irritate me."

"I will complain to Rajiya Amma."

"Go and complain. I have no issues."

He entered my room and started pulling on my blanket.

"Wake up Zeenat, wake up."

He came towards my body and started touching me and pressed my breasts. I felt extremely uncomfortable.

I opened my eyes. "What are you doing?"

"Nothing, I was just helping you so that you can wake up easily."

I wanted to slap him but I didn't. I was very angry with him and didn't want to see his face again.

As I opened my eyes, he started walking out of the room. I decided that I will talk to Rajiya Amma about him.

After half an hour, I was ready. I went down to Rajiya Amma's room and saw that she was praying.

"I want to tell you something, Amma."

"Yes, tell me what happened?"

"Dheeraj came to my room in the morning and was shouting my name."

"I know he came to your room and he was shouting your name. I even know that he was pulling on your blanket. I know everything."

"I wanted to slap him but I didn't because I wanted to share this with you first."

"Why are you so angry? Whatever he did was for your betterment. I think it is time you learn some life lessons because ultimately after two or three years, you will be facing the world. You will be meeting new people who will not like you. People hate us because we are different. You will have to adjust to them. I am not going to live with you forever; in fact, nobody lives with us till eternity.

People come and go but life does not stop. You must learn and understand all these things, my little girl."

"Ok, Rajiya Amma from tomorrow I will wake up early in the morning and take regular classes with him."

"Good and thank you, my baby, for understanding."

She gave me a hug and kissed my forehead. "Take care, baby."

I didn't know whether Amma knew everything about this morning or not. I wanted to tell her but she trusted him blindly, everyone trusted him.

I just had to wait for the right moment.

In the evening I was playing on the ground and he was staring at me. I was not comfortable whenever he was around me.

“Amma is calling you,” he said.

“I am coming.”

After few minutes I finished my game and went to Amma’s room. She was resting. I knocked on the door.

“May I come in, Amma?”

“Come in, my baby.”

"I am going out of the city for some work and will come after one month. Dheeraj will take care of the ashram and you have to help him in everything because I trust you both."

“Sure, Amma. You don't worry. I'll cooperate with him. I'll do my best.”

"I know you will not disappoint me. I trust you, my baby."

Amma started packing her luggage. I kept looking at her. She was the one who took care of me since I was 12. She had become the most important person in my life. I had learnt that there was a place called ‘Heaven’, that the world outside was vast while mine was very small. I had also learned that in the end, people will always leave you. I too wished to leave this hypocrite world, but I was still very young for it.

Amma soon left and I started taking care of everything. I was sad because I felt safe only when she was around me.

Days went by fast and he kept seeking chances to get close to me. Every day, he asked me to study with him but I denied each time. I kept doing my work.

One day, in the evening, when I was studying in my room, he barged in.

“What are you doing? Why are you not coming for studies?”

“I am busy in my other work and I didn't want to study with you. I told this thing to Amma also and I think she told you that.”

"Ok, no issues. If you don't want to study with me then I am fine with it but can you at least help me in the ashram work?"

“Yes, I'm ready to help. I assured Amma that I'll help you in every work of ashram.”

"Ok, then I will be waiting for you tomorrow."

“Ok, I'll be there.”

While this discussion was going on he put his hands on my shoulder. I felt uncomfortable but didn't utter any word because of Amma and I knew if I even said anything against him nobody will believe me.

I was waiting for the right moment.

The whole night I was busy thinking why all of this happened. Why? I cried a lot. I cursed myself, why did I take birth on this Earth. Is anything good ever going to happen to me? Is there anyone who loves me? All these questions plagued me. I couldn't sleep for many nights. I was not talking to anyone. I became a statue who had no feelings.

After spending a few days like this, one day I was working in the garden.

“Zeenat, Zeenat. Where are you?” he called.

I didn't reply. I was angry at him.

He again shouted my name. “Where are you, Zeenat?”

“Amma is asking for you. She is on the line.” When I heard these words, I started running and tears came to my eyes.

“Amma, where are you? When will you come back? How are you? I am missing you.” I cried on the phone.

"My dear baby, I am very good. I will come back after two months and I am also missing you."

"Amma, please come here as soon as possible. I don't want to live here anymore without you."

"Why? What happened?"

"Nothing much Amma. It is just that I'm missing you. You are my everything. I can't think of my life without you."

"Are you crying? Don't worry. I am always with you. I will come back soon."

She came to know that I was crying. She was neither my mother nor my relative but she had a connection with me.

"Yes, Amma. I am waiting for you. I want to sleep in your arms. I love you Amma."

"I love you too my baby. Now, you are very mature so you have to take care of everyone. I trust you."

"Yes, Amma. I will fulfill your expectations. I will take care of everything."

"Bye, my dear."

"Bye Amma."

He took the phone from me and started talking to her. I wanted to tell her many things that had been happening, but his presence made me helpless. I decided that I will wait for two months. I will wait for Amma to come and then tell her everything.

Slowly the days went by and I kept hiding from him like a thief hides from the police.

Then came another black day of my life, 14th March 2007. I woke up in the morning and started spending my time like every other day. That evening, everyone was doing Pooja in the Pooja room. I was a bit late that day. I had decided to take a bath and when I entered my room, I started changing my clothes. I turned around when I noticed sudden movement behind me and I saw him in my room. I shouted, "What are you doing? Are you mad?" Unfortunately, because of the sound of Pooja, nobody could hear me.

"There is nobody who can hear you. So, stop shouting and come here. I want to spend few moments with you. I want to sleep with you. I will give you everything. Don't worry. Come here and enjoy."

"Are you mad? What are you saying? Leave me alone!"

"Yes. I'm mad for your love. I want you. I want to sleep with you. See, you might feel bad at first but then you will enjoy it."

I did not understand. I kept yelling.

"Don't come near me."

He started coming towards me. I threw things at him. I had locked the door, I was not able to open it with my trembling hands. He started laughing and taunting me. His voice was killing me. I started running around the room, trying to get away from him.

He pushed me and I fell down on the bed. I tried to punch him but he started tying my hands with a rope.

"Please, leave me. Don't do this to me. Please, leave me."

I was crying.

He started removing his clothes and then he removed my clothes.

He raped me for more than two hours. He broke my soul into different pieces.

I was in a lot of pain. He wore his clothes and threatened to not to tell anyone or else he would show the video to everyone.

He stood and left the room. I started cursing myself. For hours, I was on the bed like a dead body. Everyone was busy in the Pooja and he joined them. After doing such a sin he was praying. I didn't get it that how can a person do this to another person.

I just wanted to die. He had played with my respect and shattered it. At night, when everyone was getting ready for dinner, I was the one lying in my room.

I was hiding from everyone because the pain was too much to bear and I was not that strong. I could still bear the physical pain but the mental pain was too much to handle. I was just praying to God to never put anyone in this hell of a situation.

As nobody had seen me from last so many hours, they started asking him about my whereabouts. I could hear their conversation but did not feel like responding.

"Dheeraj, Dheeraj. Do you know where is Zeenat?"

"I don't know. Did you check the playground or maybe she is in her room."

"We haven't seen her since evening and this is the first time she didn't come for the Pooja. We are worried about her."

"Don't worry. Everything is good. Maybe she is sleeping in her room."

"Hope so. Let's go to her room and check."

After few minutes, they started knocking my door.

"Zeenat, Zeenat. Are you there? Please open the door."

I was silent.

"Zeenat, please open the door."

I opened the door. I had covered my upper body with a shawl.

"Where were you? We were looking for you. Are you OK?"

I looked at him. He was hiding behind the door.

• • •

“Nothing has happened. I was sleeping. I am tired. Sorry I didn't attend the Pooja today.”

“That is ok. We were just worried about you. We also asked Dheeraj but he also had no idea where you went.”

“I'm fine. Don't worry. I need rest. I want to sleep some more.”

“Please eat some food. You are our responsibility.”

“I don't want to eat anything. If I feel hungry, I'll eat. Don't worry. Right now I need to rest.”

“Ok fine. If you need any help just let us know.”

“Ok.”

I locked the door again. I was crying internally. I was recalling those beautiful moments which I had spent with Amma. I spent whole night like this.

I kept to my room the next few days. I just wanted to leave this world. I couldn’t think of anything good that ever happened to me. I decided that I'll tell everything to everyone though I knew that nobody would believe me still I wanted to speak out loud.

That the evening, everyone was waiting for me for the Pooja but I was hiding in my room. They were shouting my name. So, I decided to come out of the room.

“See, Zeenat is coming,” they shouted.

I smiled.

“The whole day you have been sleeping in your room. Is everything ok?”

“Yes, everything is good. I just wanted to spend some time alone.”

“I want to tell you all something but let's start with the Pooja first,” I said.

• • •

I looked around him but he was not there. After finishing with the Pooja, I started distributing Prasad to everyone.

“Where is Dheeraj?” I asked.

“We don't know. We haven't seen him since afternoon.”

“Ok.”

“Zeenat, you wanted to tell us something. What happened? Is it anything serious?”

“Yes, something but I'll tell you tomorrow.”

“Okay.”

"Can you do me a favor? Please send dinner to my room as I'll not be able to come."

"Sure! We will give it to you in your room."

"Thank you, everyone."

So, I went to my room. I was thinking about Dheeraj. I wanted to tell everything to everyone in front of him. I'll talk to everyone tomorrow morning.

As I reached my room and switched on the lights, I saw him lying on my bed.

“What are you doing here?”

“Nothing, I was just waiting for you. I wanted to spend some time with you.”

“Tomorrow I'll tell everything to everyone.”

“Go and tell. Just remember nobody will trust you. Everyone respects me. So, you will be wasting your and everyone’s time.”

“You might be right. Nobody will believe me but I trust Amma, she will definitely listen to me, she loves me.”

“Ok. Do whatever you want to do.”

As soon as I went to open the door, he came from behind and held me tightly in his arms.

“Leave me,” I screamed in anger.

He pushed me and I fell down on the bed. I remembered how his arms were coming towards my jeans.

I kicked his private part and pushed him. I opened the door and started calling everyone.

After few seconds I heard the voice of some footsteps. Three people were coming towards my room. I was crying.

“What happened, Zeenat?” they asked.

“He came to my room and started touching me. He tried to rape me.” I kept on repeating.

“Are you mad? What are you saying? Do you even know who he is?”

“I know each and everything and I'm not mad. I know you all trust him but he tried to rape me.”

"You do not seem fine from last two-three days. You are talking rubbish; nobody is going to believe you. Go and take some rest."

“I will tell all this to Amma, she trusts me.”

“Ok, you can do whatever you want to do but for now please respect the reputation of this ashram and you need not say anything to others.”

I was feeling helpless; I had no other option but to stay silent for some time.

“Ok.”

“I told you nobody would believe you. I'm the head of this place. I can do whatever I want. I don’t fear anyone. So, don't behave like a kid and just enjoy these moments. I will come tomorrow again and we will enjoy.”

He banged the door as he left.

•••

His words kept on resonating in my mind. How can a person destroy other person's life just to fulfill their sexual needs? Now, I had to leave this place as soon as possible.

I was lying on the bed and it was midnight. I wanted to sleep but his words kept coming back. The insult of Ashram's people, the way they treated me as if I was the one committing a sin? All these things gave me a new lesson. I had started thinking that the Ashram's people were my family but now they gave me another reason to hate the world.

The next morning while I was on my bed, I heard a voice. Dheeraj was shouting my name.

"Zeenat, Zeenat."

"Yes, what happened?"

"There is a call for you come fast."

"Ok, I'm coming."

"Hello," I answered the call.

"Hello baby," Amma was on the other side.

"Amma, how are you?"

"I'm fine, baby."

"When are you coming back?"

"I'm coming back by tomorrow. Don't worry."

"Amma, I want to share so many things with you. Please come back as soon as possible. I can't live without you. You are my everything."

"Yes, baby. I will be there tomorrow. Don't worry. You have so many people in the Ashram. Everyone loves you, especially Dheeraj. He was saying that you are helping him take care of the Ashram. I am proud of you, baby."

"Amma nobody is good. Everyone is selfish here."

The moment I said these words he took the phone from my hand and started talking.

"Zeenat go and get ready for the Pooja. Everyone is waiting for you," he said.

"Ok, I'm going."

He wanted to show Amma how he was taking care of me but he didn't know that after today he will be thrown out of this ashram.

I went to my room. Now I just had to wait until tomorrow. I took a bath and had breakfast. After that, I went to the garden. He was watching me. So many things had happened to me but I was happy because tomorrow Amma was coming.

I decided that I'll tell her everything. I knew she will trust me.

As I was playing, he came to me. "I know you are very happy because Amma is coming tomorrow but you dare not say anything to her otherwise you will have to face the consequences," he tried to threaten me. I just ignored him because I wanted justice. Hours were going by fast.

The next afternoon, I was waiting for her. I came to know that she would be here within two hours. So, I went to my room to take some rest.

My sleep was interrupted as I heard Dheeraj's voice, he was shouting my name.

"Zeenat, Zeenat come here."

"What happened? Why are you shouting my name?"

He was crying while was talking to someone on phone.

"Amma is no more," he said between sobs.

"What gibberish are you talking?" I was stunned.

I took the phone from his hands.

"Hello. What happened?" I.

"We are calling from Delhi City Hospital. We have one patient name Rajiya Amma and she is no more. Kindly come and collect the dead body."

I was silent for some time. I couldn't digest what they just said.

Dheeraj took the phone from my hands.

"Yes, we are coming. We will be there in a couple of hours," he replied.

I fell to the ground.

After few hours, I saw myself lying on the bed. Everyone was looking at me.

I started shouting, "Amma, Amma.

"Where is she? I want to go Delhi. I want to meet her. Please leave me. Please."

"Dheeraj has gone to bring her. He will be coming soon. Please try to understand, she is not with us anymore. She is dead. Now, you both have to take care of this Ashram. Everyone is depending on you," they all tried to calm me down."

I had no words. I just wanted to be left alone to cry. This time again God had given me wounds that could never heal. After all that had happened, this was the last stroke, I just wanted to die.

I knew I had to take care of this Ashram as this was her last wish but how could I live where nobody understood me? If I live here, he will rape me every day. I needed to make a decision. Amma had opened this Ashram. Everyone depended on her but now it is my responsibility to take care of everything.

I realized that I have no other option but to spend my whole life here for them. I had to fulfill Amma's dreams. The next evening, I was in the garden and saw him coming with a big coffin. As I saw this, I started running towards him. As he laid the coffin and opened it, I peeked inside. Amma was sleeping, her eyes were closed. I shouted her name but she did not reply. I wanted to listen to her voice, her words, especially "My baby".

Somehow I had realized the bitter truth of life i.e. death. She taught me so many things. Now I will walk on her path.

Since morning everyone was coming to Ashram to see her one last time. It was her wish that when she dies, her body should be buried within the boundaries of the Ashram. So, everyone was working towards that.

The time came Dheeraj held the coffin and we buried the body in the soil. People were crying but I felt like had no emotions left with me.

In the evening, the whole Ashram was silent. Everyone was in a sad mood. Days passed but nothing changed because she was the only parent everyone had. People loved her.

After two weeks of the incident, people started working. In the morning, as I was coming from my room, I saw Dheeraj talking to someone. He was new. I hid behind a door and started listening to their conversation.

“What are you doing here?” Dheeraj asked him.

“I need the rest of my money. I have been calling you since last one week but your phone was switched off,” the other person replied in anger.

“Here, things are not good. Try to understand. I will give you your money as soon as possible.”

"I don't know anything. Give me my money, otherwise, you will have to face the consequences. In our work, payments must be made in time."

“I know, but please understand here the conditions what I am trying to say. I have to withdraw the money from the Ashram's account which is not possible right now.”

“I am not taking any excuses; I need my money within three days. I am staying at the Ganga Lounge. I will come after three days.”

"Ok. I will arrange for something but please don't come here again. I will send the money to your lounge or I will come personally there."

“Ok, but remember one thing… you have only three days,” the person left after warning Dheeraj. I understood that Dheeraj has to pay a big amount to him because he did some work for him. I wanted to know about the work because Dheeraj was going to pay money from the Ashram's account which is opened to use for only Ashram's work and I was afraid that now in the absence of Amma he will misuse the money.

After the end of the conversation, Dheeraj started walking towards my room. I rushed towards the kitchen.

I was looking for some spices in the kitchen when he came and held me from the back.

“What are you doing here?” he asked.

“Leave me.” I tried escaping.

“Amma is no more. Everyone trusts me. Now, I can do anything with you. Nobody is going to stop me.”

I thought that after Amma's death, he may have learnta lesson but he was still a moron who wanted to spoil other’s lives. I pushed him and left. I wanted to expose him as I knew that something bad was going on in the Ashram. So, I decided that I'll monitor his activities. I waited for the day when he will go to meet that person and soon the day came. He came out from his room with a black bag in his right hand. He was going outside. I started following him. As I reached the gate, the security guard stopped me.

“Where are you going?” the guards asked me.

“I wanted to buy some spices for the kitchen,” I lied.

“Don’t you know it is not allowed for children to go outside the Ashram?”

"I know but it is important right now. Everyone is busy with their work. Please let me go. I'll come as soon as possible."

“Okay. Go and come fast.”

“Thank you very much.”

I started running. After fifteen minutes, he stopped as he saw that other person. They started talking.

“Here take your money and now, leave this place,” Dheeraj instructed the guy.

“Ok, I will be leaving this place today. But I want to know one thing she loved you, she gave all her money to you, so why did you get her killed?” the guy questioned Dheeraj.

"This is none of your business. You have done my work and now I have made the payment. So from now on, we don't know each other."

With this, they both left the place.

The moment I heard those words why you killed her, I was totally shocked. Dheeraj murdered Amma. He hired that person to murder Amma. So, many questions were arising in my mind. I wanted to kill him but I was feeling helpless.

I went to Ashram. I wanted to tell this to everyone. I wanted to kill him but I knew no one would believe me, they all trusted him blindly. I started following him so, that I can get any proof and I can prove him guilty.

One day, I was doing some work in the garden. He came to me.

“I am watching you from the last few days. You are noticing my every activity. Stop these things,” he said to me in anger.

"I am not noticing you," I replied innocently.

"Don't lie. I saw you."

"Think what you want to think. I don't care."

"Ok, you don't care. I will see you at night then."

"What will you do? Will you rape me again like you did earlier?"

I started shouting at him.

"Will you rape me? Will you rape?"

"Are you mad? What are you doing?"

"No, I'm not mad."

"Then stop this nonsense."

Everyone came from their rooms hearing our argument.

"What is going on here?" they asked.

"Nothing, she is mad. She is shouting that I raped her," he said.

"Zeenat, why are you doing all this?"

"Because I am telling the truth. He raped me that night I told this thing to all of you. Now, he was saying that he will rape me again. He killed Amma also. He is her murderer."

"Are you mad? What the hell are you saying? He loves her. He can never murder her."

"I know the real truth. If you all don't believe me right now wait I will prove it to you all."

"Take her to her room. She has gone mad. She is ruining the atmosphere of the Ashram." Dheeraj shouted.

Four people came to me and started pushing me towards the room. I kept shouting that he was a murderer but no one paid any heed to me.

They locked me in the room.

• • •

“Now, shout in the room and talk with walls. You will not get food for the whole day. This is your punishment,” he said.

“Ok, I don’t care. You do whatever you want to do,” I said furiously.

I was sad inside. Because now I will not be able to find any proof against him.

In the afternoon, I was lying on my bed. I heard few people talking to Dheeraj; I could hear the conversation very clearly.

“She is creating problems every day. Yesterday few people were talking about Amma’s death and even they were asking this thing to our ashram people,” the person said.

"You are right, Atul. Every day she is creating a problem for everyone. We should do something," Dheeraj replied.

Ah, so this other person’s name is Atul. I made a mental note of his name and facial features, if in case I needed to recollect it later.

“But what?” Atul asked.

“I don’t know but don’t worry I will arrange something for her like we arranged for Amma.”

“Okay. She is locked in her room and has no idea that what is going to happen to her,” Atul said with an evil laugh.

“Yes, don’t worry. Everything will be according to our plan.”

They both started laughing and their voices were irritating me. I realized that I’m not safe here. I have to leave the place as soon as possible but I had no idea that where should I go.

As I started to back out, they saw me. I tried to rush, but they were faster. They took me by my arms and locked me in a room.

I was thinking about a place where I can go and live happily. Suddenly a thought hit me, one day Amma had mentioned a friend's café in New Delhi. She had said that whenever I want to go outside for work I should go to her friend's café. Now, how to escape from this place? They have locked me and now everyone's watching my activities. It was impossible to run from this place but I wanted to go because I knew if I stay here they would kill me.

After two days my punishment was over. Now, I could come out of my room and talk to people. I kept planning and waiting for the right time to escape from this place. That evening, I was working in my room. He came and started talking about random things.

I kept ignoring him but again and again, he shouted my name.

"Are you ignoring me?" he asked.

"Zeenat, are you ignoring me?" he asked again with anger.

"I don't want to talk to you. So, please get out of my room."

"This is my ashram. This is my room. You are also mine. I have full rights on you. I can do anything with you like I did on that night."

"Yes, I remember everything. But mark my words one day I'll definitely take revenge for Amma's murder and for my rape too."

"Hahaha... Really?" he laughed loudly.

"I know you also enjoyed that night and I didn't kill Amma. Nobody has any proof of that, she died in an accident. Everyone believes that."

"Yes, everyone knows this but this is not the reality. I don't have any proof right now but one day I'll take revenge on you."

"Baby, you do that. Do what you want to do but please come here now and enjoy the evening."

• • •

He locked the door. He started walking towards me. This time, I did not feel scared of him because I knew that he can do only one thing. He can rape me and that was not new for me because now I was fighting with god for everything. My fight was with god and not with him anymore.

He laid his hands on my neck and then my back. I kept sitting silently because I knew if I shouted all people would blame me.

He held me in his hands and threw me on the bed. He started taking off his clothes. He came to me and started groping my whole body.

My soul was asking so many questions to God but God replied to none. Again someone played with my soul, broke me into small pieces and left me to live in this world.

“Don’t try telling this to anyone because nobody trusts you.”

He left the room as I lay on the bed with torn clothes.

I heard about rapes in newspapers so many times but I discovered real pain when it happened to me. I should salute the rape victim-survivors for their courage, for their strength. They are an inspiration to everyone.

I cried whole night not because I was raped by someone but because I couldn't send him to jail for Amma's murder.

The next morning, I behaved like nothing had happened. After planning for the whole day, I came to know that a function was going to be organized by the Ashram next week on Wednesday. I just had to wait for that day.

Finally, the day came, I woke up in the morning at 10. I pretended to work as usual so no one would have any doubts.

“What are you doing here?” Dheeraj asked.

“I'm just doing my work,” I replied.

“Today night I'll come to your room. We will enjoy.”

I didn't reply and continued doing my work silently. Shortly after, I went to my room and started packing. I took my bag, covered my face, and started walking. I feared for my life. I mixed with the crowd and headed to the main gate. I hoped no one was there. I saw two people talking near the gate. I hid and started waiting for them to leave from there.

After few minutes, they left and I crossed the main gate. I turned and looked at the Ashram one last time, the place where I spent most of the time, where I had someone in my life who cared for me. I wanted to live my whole life in the Ashram but you cannot always get what you want.

"Sometimes we want to spend our life according to our wishes, but situations don't support us. We then have to adjust our lives according to the situations."

I started walking. It was the first time I was alone at night. People were looking at me with doubtful eyes. I was scared but behaved as if I knew what I was doing.

New Journey of Life Starts

I hired an auto for bus stand. I had no clue how I would arrange things but I had faith in myself.

When I reached the bus stand, I stepped out of the auto and took few steps. It was very crowded.

I remembered Amma's words: Zeenat, a time will come when you would have to come out of your comfort zone and stand for yourself.

One bus was parked.

"Bhaiya, is this bus going to Patna?" I asked.

"Yes," the bus conductor replied.

"How much time will it take?"

"Maximum three and a half hours."

"Please give me a ticket for the full journey," I requested.

He gave me one ticket and I paid him the money which I had stolen from Dheeraj's room.

I entered the bus. Eighty percent was filled with males. I felt scared. I remembered Amma, took a deep breath and sat on my seat. I feared that when Dheeraj finds out that I had escaped, he will definitely look for me. After few minutes driver started the bus. I looked back at the Ashram and recollected all good things that had happened.

I didn't know where I was going, where I would be staying, but I had a hope of new life. One lady was sitting next to me. She was staring me. I pretended to sleep. I knew that she wanted to talk to me but I didn't want to talk to anyone.

"Where are you going?

I didn't reply.

She repeated, "Where are you going?"

"I am going to Patna," I replied.

"What is your name?"

"My name is Eknoor," I lied.

She was stared at my clothes. After one and a half hour, we reached Patna. I hired an auto and instructed the driver to drive towards the railway station. From there, I booked one general ticket for a train to Delhi.

After waiting for an hour finally the train arrived at the station. I entered the general compartment. Many people were standing in the compartment. Everyone was pushing each other and trying to make the place for themselves. I took a few steps to stand in one corner.

"Why God has sent me into this world?" I asked myself.

I remember Amma's words, what she used to tell me whenever I cried, I know you have faced a lot in your life, you have gone through the worst phases but the good things are waiting for us at the end. So, don't be sad and there are many other people who also have faced so much in their life still, they are living their life because they have faith in God. Be an inspiration for other people. You can also become someone's hope but first just find yourself.

These words gave me a reason to live life happily. I started hoping for a better future. After waiting and standing for long, the train finally reached New Delhi railway station at 1 in the afternoon. As I exited the train, I realized two people were following me and they were talking about a brothel. I felt uncomfortable so I started walking fast and after few minutes I saw an exit board sign. I started walking towards the exit.

"Hello, where are you going?" one of the guys who was following me asked.

I didn't reply. They started following me again and suddenly he pushed me and put his hand on my neck. “I asked you where you are going. I think you are new here. I can drop you, just tell me where you want to go.”

They started discussing with each other. I was unable to understand them but I had this feeling that something was not right.

"*Jawan hai, Aacha maal hai. Aacha paisa milega. Time mat lgao, le chalo ise yhan se*."

I pushed them and started running. After few minutes I realized that they were not following me. I relaxed and started looking for an auto. After waiting for almost half an hour, an auto came to me.

“Ma'am, where do you want to go?" the auto - driver asked.

"I want to go Connaught Place," I replied.

"Okay."

He started auto. I wondered if they would give me work or not?

"Ma'am, are you new here?"

"Yes," I replied.

"Okay."

After fifteen minutes I reached Benz Cafe. I had heard that it is a famous cafe. Amma had once told me that when I turned eighteen, she would send me to Delhi to work at this café. She was not with me anymore and I had to do something for myself.

We are God's own creatures. God gives each one of us an opportunity; we must understand his sign and take full advantage of it. God has knocked my door. I entered in Benz Cafe. I saw four girls and three boys working there. Everyone wore the same colored dress.

"Can I meet Umar Sheikh?" I asked.

"Yes, but who are you?" the receptionist as she gave an inquisitive look.

"My name is Zeenat. I have come from Gaya, Bihar. I'm Rajiya Amma's daughter," I answered proudly.

Everyone was looking at me, at my dirty clothes and dirty sneakers. Also, everyone was talking in English while I was talking in Bihari.

A person came out from the staff room.

"Who are you? What do you want?" he asked.

"I want to meet Umar Sheikh. I have come from Bihar," I repeated.

"Please leave this place. He is not here. You can meet him tomorrow," he replied rudely.

"Ok," I said.

I had no other option so I went outside and waited for him. I was really hungry as I hadn't eaten since I had escaped. The café was crowded.

Every time we cannot blame our destiny for everything. I knew I had to make my destiny.

I was not feeling well; my head was paining.

One boy came to me and offered me some coins, "Take it, go and eat something."

I didn't reply.

I heard a voice coming from the other side.

"Rajveer, come here. Why are you wasting your time with her?" a girl called from inside.

"I'm coming. Wait for a few minutes," he shouted back.

He kept staring at me.

• • •

Suddenly, the girl came and held his arm.

"Rajveer, let's go. Everyone is waiting for you," she insisted.

"Why are you staring at her?"

"What are you doing here? Get lost from here. You people come from other cities and start begging," she said to me.

I was just listening to her words because I was helpless.

"Manager! Come here. What the hell is she doing here?" she called out again.

"You are still here? I told you to get lost from this place," the manager shouted as he came out.

"I am waiting for Umar Sheikh. I want to meet him," I requested.

“Guards! Come here and throw her out," he ordered.

Guards came and pushed me towards the road. I fell to the ground.

"What the hell are you doing guys?" Rajveer asked.

"She is a girl. We should respect her. Hey, you, manager, you go inside. You also leave Shanaya, I want to talk to her.”

"No, I'm not going anywhere," Shanaya said.

"Please, Shanaya try to understand the situation. I’ll join you in five minutes." Shanaya left and Rajveer came to me to help me get up.

"I don't know anything about you but something attracted me towards you. Why do you want to meet Umar Sheikh? What is your relationship with him? Tell me so that I can help you."

"My name is Zeenat. I am from Bihar. He is my mother's friend. She died in an accident. She told me that when I'll be eighteen years she will send me to Delhi for work. I have come here to fulfill that dream of hers.”

"Ok, so you have come here for work but Umar uncle is not here right now. He will come in the evening, so, you can come in the evening and meet him."

"Ok, thank you."

"Here, take these five hundred rupees, go to that shop and eat something," he said pointing at a shop nearby.

"No, no I cannot take this money. We don't know each other and still, you are doing so much for me. Why?" I asked.

"You don't think about that, just take this money and go and have some food."

He pushed the money into my hands and started walking towards the cafe. I kept looking in his direction, unable to understand why he was helping me. Why was he doing so much for me? Nobody gave me this much importance, except Amma.

I went to the shop for some food. Here as well, I attracted attention so I quickly took some food and started going towards the cafe. I saw Rajveer's car coming out from the cafe parking.

I didn't know him but I wanted to talk to him. I wanted to share my problems with him. I kept waiting for Umar uncle outside the cafe. After two hours a car entered the Café parking.

A man came out of the car. Somehow, I knew that he was Umar Sheikh.

"Umar Sheikh Uncle?" I called out.

"Yes, who are you?" he answered.

"My name is Zeenat. I am from Gaya. I was living in Rajiya Amma's ashram. She told me about you. She told me to come and meet you for a job."

"Oh! She is a good friend. I knew her since school days," he seemed ecstatic.

"I know. She always talked about you."

"Why are you standing there? Come with me."

As soon as I entered the café, everyone was looking at me. They were shocked to see me especially the manager who insulted me and threw me out.

We went to a room and Uncle started talking about his and Amma's memories. Suddenly he asked me about Amma.

"Where is Rajiya? Why she did not come with you?"

"She is no more. She died in an accident."

"What? When did this happen?"

"It's a long story. I want to tell you so many things but this is not the right time. Umar uncle, I came here for work. She told me that you will help me in Delhi."

"Don't worry, beti, I'll help you. You are my friend's favourite daughter, she always talked about you."

"Thank you uncle, I know I'm asking a lot from you but I have no place to stay and don't even have enough cash with me."

"That is ok, dear. You can stay at my place with me and my wife."

"I am really thankful to you for everything."

"I am not doing anything for you. When you Amma came here, I had promised I'll help you whenever you need it." He said.

"You are so kind and this is your generosity that even though she is not with us you're still willing to fulfill your promise," I replied.

"Perhaps, but she always helped me in my life, both financially and non-financially, and I never forget the ones who help me."

"We are social animals. We substantially forget the generosity of other people who helped us in our worst situations and then again we expect their helping hands for us."

"Yes, you're absolutely right but there are few people in our lives who we never forget because they have done so much for us." He said.

"I agree with you. I am also waiting for those people because in my childhood my parents left me and when I started living life happily with Amma, she left me alone in this world. God took her away from me."

"Just wait for the right moment, my dear, the right person will come in your life and take away all your tears and problems from your life."

"I have no faith in God. He has never done anything good in my life. He always made my life miserable."

"We are God's children, he can never do bad to us and when he does that is because he has something better planned for us."

"Maybe you are right, but I have never seen anything good happen to me. Earlier, I just wanted to die, but then I realized that I yet have so much to achieve in life."

"Thank god that you have realized the real meaning of life. Suicide is not a solution to any problem in life."

"Yes, I have realized the real meaning of life now, I want to do something for myself and fulfill my Amma's wishes. We have to fight those problems. We shouldn't make any decision based on a few experiences. There are so many people in this world who are facing many problems as compared to us, but they never give up, they fight through it, fall on the ground, stand up, fight again and eventually they win."

"Yes, you are right. Amma always said the same; you both have same views on life."

"Yes, we do, but she was doing an amazing job with the orphanage. She had an inspiring philosophy towards life. Since the very early days, she wanted to do something for the society. Her parents left her, the society didn't accept her and they criticized her in every possible manner. But, each time she took the criticism positively and worked on improving herself. She proved everyone wrong with her work. She gave hope to youngsters. She became their father and mother.

"Yes, she gave hope to many youngsters like me. Even when my parents left me in front of the ashram she was the one who accepted me, she was the one who took care of me like her own child."

"We have been talking for so long, and I didn't even offer you food. Sorry daughter."

"No need to say sorry. I'm not feeling hungry; I had food a few hours ago. I wanted to meet you so as I was sitting outside and waiting for you, and I had food from outside only."

"Why were you sitting outside? Why were you not waiting inside?" he asked.

"When I came to the café and enquired about you, the manager told me that you will come tomorrow and didn't allow me to sit inside. I had to wait outside the café. He insulted me there too. So, that's why I was waiting on the footpath." I answered.

"Seriously, I don't believe this. Ajay! Ajay come here," he shouted.

"Yes, Sir!" Ajay said as he entered the room.

"Did she come to our cafe? Did you insult her? Tell me, I want to know the truth."

"Sir, I didn't know anything about her. Sorry, Sir." Ajay pleaded.

"Don't say sorry to me. Do you know who is she? She is the daughter of my best friend. She came from Gaya to meet me and you insulted her. She was waiting for me, sitting on the footpath, only because of you. If you really want to say sorry then you should say sorry to her. If she forgives you, I'll forgive you too."

"Sorry, ma'am for everything. I didn't do anything intentionally. Please forgive me. I was just doing my job."

"It is ok. You are elder than me. Please don't say sorry. You were doing your job, I understand." I said.

"Thank you so much, ma'am."

"Never disrespect anyone because nobody knows when the time will change," I said.

"Yes, ma'am I understand. I won't repeat my mistake," Ajay said apologetically.

"Ajay, go and bring two burgers and coffee for us," Uncle ordered.

"Yes, Sir. Just give me ten minutes," he left to bring our order.

"Rajiya had not given you birth but you think just like her. I am impressed."

"Thank you, Umar uncle. I just want to fulfill her dreams. I wish to develop the Ashram further."

"I know you will fulfill her dreams but first you need to develop yourself. You should do something for yourself."

"You're right and that's the reason I came here. I want to work here. I want to learn something from you."

"Don't worry about work. You have just come here, so enjoy for few days and after that, I'll give you work."

"No Umar uncle, I have come here only for work. You just tell me my work. I'll not disappoint you."

"I am elder to you and I'm your Amma's best friend, you must comply with my orders."

"Ok, Umar uncle," I said as I laughed.

"Sir, May I come in?" Ajay asked.

"Yes, come in."

He served coffee and burgers gently. I knew that he didn't say sorry from his heart but I also didn't want to destroy the atmosphere of the cafe so I accepted his sorry.

"Thank you, Ajay," I said.

"Welcome, ma'am."

"Zeenat, I think we should leave now because it's too late. They have to close the cafe and my wife is also waiting for me," said Uncle as he looked at his watch.

"Yes, uncle you are right. We have been talking for last five hours."

"Give me fifteen minutes and after that, we will go."

"Ok Uncle. I'm waiting for you outside the café."

I pushed the door and went outside the café, waiting for him. After many days I felt happy. Somehow Rajveer's face came in front of my eyes again and again.

"Zeenat, come let's go." Uncle arrived and started walking towards his car.

Uncle was very talkative. He only needed a person to talk. His conversations went on and on.

"Zeenat, we don't have a girl. I only have one son. We always prayed to Allah for a daughter but that was not what he planned for us. My wife will be very happy to see you."

"Umar uncle. I did not get the love of father and mother from my parents still Amma loved me more than my parents but now she is also not with me. When the first time I saw you, I was scared but when I started talking to you I felt good. Now I am excited to meet your wife. I'll always stand up to your expectations."

"Do you know the first time I saw you, I saw my friend's shadow in you. You have all qualities which Rajiya had. Zeenat, you are going to my home, you will be living there. I hope you are comfortable with this or should I arrange some other place for you where you can live independently?"

"Don't say such things, Umar uncle. I'm happy and very comfortable. I'm happy that God is giving me an opportunity to start a life again with a beautiful family."

"You are a doll, dear. Thank you."

•••

Part-1

We reached Umar uncle's home in fifteen minutes. He knocked the door and after few seconds his wife came to open the door. As we entered, Uncle hugged her warmly.

"Fatima, how are you?"

"I'm fine," she replied.

"How was your day? Was everything good?"

"Yes, it was good."

"Where is Shoaib?"

"He has gone to a party and will come after 10."

"Fatima, meet Zeenat, my childhood friend Rajiya's daughter."

She came towards me, touched my face, and gave me a tight hug. I teared up. She kissed me on my forehead.

"I don't know much about you but the moment I hugged you, I felt great. You will stay here with us, beti."

"Fatima, I'm going to my room. Please show Zeenat her room."

"Ok dear."

She held my hand and took me to a room on the second floor.

"Zeenat, this is your room. You will stay here. If you need anything just tell me, please don't hesitate."

"Yes aunty and thank you so much for everything."

"You are like my daughter. God didn't give me an opportunity to become the mother of a daughter but after meeting you I can say he has fulfilled my wish. From now on, you're my daughter."

"I'm lost for words. You both love me so much. I have never experienced this much love from anyone, except Amma. Even my parents left me when I was twelve. They left me, maybe according to them I was a burden but I would want to meet them and ask them some questions if I get a chance."

"You have so much hate in your heart for your parents. This is not a good thing. Anyway, I'll not lecture you on this topic because you have suffered a lot and I can understand. You go freshen up and take rest, after two hours I'll call you for dinner."

"Ok, thank you."

She went from the room. I closed the door and looked around. It was a beautiful room. I was felt happy as after many years something good was happening with me. With a deep contented sigh, I started unpacking my luggage.

I didn't know why but Rajveer's face kept coming in front of my eyes. I wanted to meet him again that's why I was waiting eagerly to start working in the cafe.

"Zeenat, Zeenat, come daughter. We are waiting for you. Dinner is ready," Fatima aunty called from downstairs.

"Coming!"

Aunty had pulled me a chair that was adjacent to hers, "Zeenat this is your chair. Now, you're a part of our family."

"Wow! You guys are showering me with so much love. I have never got this much respect and love from anyone. I'm not habituated to such things."

"Beti, we're not doing anything extra. We're selfish. We were wishing for a daughter and now God has sent you in our life. So, it's our responsibility to take care of you."

I stood and hugged her tightly.

We finished our dinner with smiles on our faces.

"Today, we'll play carom," Fatima Aunty announced.

"I love the game!" Uncle replied with excitement.

"Zeenat, do you know how to play it?" aunty asked.

"Yes, I also love this game," I said.

We started playing and I won the first game.

"We had been waiting for this life for a really long time and finally you made our dream come true. I have kept all the necessary things in your room, you can check and still if you need anything you can tell me without hesitating. We're here for you." Fatima aunty said. I noticed she was getting emotional.

"You both have done so much for me; I don't deserve all of this love and care. I'm a girl of an orphanage whose parents left her in the childhood. These things mean a lot. I am scared of being this happy because whenever someone comes into my life and loves me this much, God eventually takes them away. I don't want to lose you both." I said.

"We understand your situation dear. We will never leave you. Don't worry. I know you have faced so much in your life, forget everything and let's embark on this new journey together. A new life is waiting for you and I know it would be hard for you to forget the past, but you should try."

"You're right. But would take some time."

"Take your time but try to enjoy your life now."

"I promise I will try. I'm feeling sleepy; may I go to my room?" I asked.

"Yes, go and have a good sleep. Good night, my daughter."

"Good night."

I went to my room. I closed the door and switched off the lights.

I was lying on the bed and thinking about my future. I knew I had to avenge Amma's murder. I wanted to meet Dheeraj and ask him why he did he do it. Somehow, I felt he had murdered Amma just because of me; he knew that if I told her about his actions, she would have definitely punished him.

Before closing eyes to sleep, I decided that I'll wake up early and help Fatima aunt in the kitchen.

The next day, I woke up at 5:30, performed my morning rituals, and exactly at 6:00 a.m, I went downstairs. I saw Fatima aunty working in the kitchen.

She was surprised to see me. "What are you doing here so early, Zeenat?"

"I used to wake up early in the morning even in the Ashram and also I wanted to help you."

"No dear. I can manage you don't need to wake up early in the morning. You're like our daughter. Even your uncle will not allow this thing."

"I knew that you'll not allow me. Seriously, I really want to help you. Even in the ashram, I used to help in the kitchen. I love cooking and people say that I cook really tasty food."

"I also know that you are very stubborn. Ok, if you want to help me in the kitchen then you can, but first, you would need to take permission from your uncle. If he allows you, then I have no problem."

"Okay. Can I help you now?"

"Yes, you can."

"So, what are we preparing for breakfast today?"

"Nothing special just your uncle's favorite dish, 'Poori - Aloo'."

"Oh! I also love it and I can cook it very well."

"That's nice. Let's first cook the Sabzi; we'll cook the Pooris when everyone is on the dining table to serve it hot."

"Ok."

Eventhough this was my first morning in their house, I felt like I've been living here for past many years.

"We are done with the preparations, so now go and have some rest. You are very young and this is not good for your health."

"Ok, Aunty."

I went to my room. Actually, I was feeling a little sleepy. As I fell asleep, I thought about talking to uncle for joining work. Moreover, I wanted to talk to him. I knew he belonged to a rich family still, his yesterday's behavior fascinated me and made me fall for him. Now, I just wanted to know more about him.

Sometimes we don't expect anything from God, but he sends someone in our life and that person starts changing our life.

I woke up and looked for my watch; it was 11:30. I washed my face and went to the lobby area. Fatima aunty was reading a newspaper. I looked around for Umar uncle as I wanted to discuss a few things with him.

"Fatima aunty, where is Umar uncle?"

"He is not here. He went to the café."

"Oh! I wanted to discuss few work-related things with him."

"Don't worry. You just came yesterday and you want to discuss work so soon. Take rest and enjoy the beautiful city today. After that you can go to work, I won't say a word."

"Ok, where are we going today?"

"We are going to Sarojini Market for shopping."

"Oh! Great! I have never shopped for myself. This will be my first time."

"Do not worry, I'll be with you. For now, I'll help you and guide you in everything."

I was excited.

"Now go and get ready. I'll prepare your breakfast. After that, we'll leave for shopping."

I went to my room for getting ready. I was unable to understand the turn my life had taken. A few days ago, I was living in an ashram, was raped and spurned by the society.

As soon as I got ready, I went to the lobby and saw Fatima aunty frying pooris for me.

"Can I help you, aunty?"

"No, you just sit there."

After a few minutes, she came with my breakfast. Everything looked so yummy. In the orphanage, I could not made food of my choice, this was the first time I tasted such yummy food, I loved it!

I took the first bite and it was really very yummy. I ate more than six pooris within ten minutes.

"Can you do me a favor, Aunty?"

"Yes?"

"Can I kiss your hands? The pooris and, especially, the sabzi were really yummy."

"Hahaha, don't say such things. I'm not a professional chef."

"No, everything is really very tasty. Can you teach me how to cook?"

"Yes, sure I'll teach you, but now I'm going to get ready because we're getting late for shopping."

She went to her room.

Suddenly, I heard someone knocking the door. A boy in his early twenties was standing there. As I opened the door, he started shouting.

“Mom, mom... Where are you? Mom, are you listening to me?"

"Yes, beta. I'm coming, just give me five minutes," Aunty replied from her room.

"Who are you?" he asked, looking at me.

"My name is Zeenat. I have come from Bihar."

As I was introducing myself, Fatima aunty entered.

"How are you beta? Where were you last night? Your father was waiting for you the whole night."

"Mom, I was busy. Leave that, I'm really hungry. Please give me some food."

"Ok, my dear son, just give me ten minutes. I'll bring you poori and sabzi."

"No, I don't want to eat poori and sabzi. You know I don't eat oily food. Give me juice, bread, and eggs."

"Oh! Sorry, my son. I forgot; I'll bring you your favorite food. Wait for ten minutes."

I went to the kitchen and started helping Fatima Aunt.

"My son, meet her. She is Zeenat, your papa's best friend daughter.”

"Hello, my name is Shoaib."

"Hello," I replied.

"I have some work in my room so, I'm going. You both talk to each other." Aunty went to her room leaving us alone.

"So, why did you come from Bihar? I mean you wanted to visit Delhi or did you come here for some other purpose?" he asked.

"Actually, I left my house. I have come to find some work and I'll be living here."

"Ok."

"What discussion is going on guys?" Aunty said as she entered the room all ready to leave.

"Nothing special, mom."

"Okay, my son. We are already late. Zeenat, come, lets' go."

"Yes, aunty. I'm ready. "

"Mom, where are you going?"

"We are going to Sarojini Bazaar for shopping. We will be back before 5 in the evening."

"Okay, mom. I'm going to my friend's house. I will come back tomorrow."

"Every day you do this and I allow you. I never ask you anything, but now if you want to stay at your friend's place, you have to take permission from your father."

"Mom, this is not right. For everything, I have to take his permission. I'm not a child; I'm twenty-one years old."

"I don't want to argue on this matter, moreover, I don't have time for all this nonsense. If you want to stay at your friend's house, you have to take his permission, as simple as that."

"Okay, fine. I'll take the permission."

"Good. Now, we're leaving. I have made your fruit salad and it is in the refrigerator if you feel hungry you can have it."

"Okay, mom."

We left the place and hired an auto-rickshaw from our home. I had not heard about this famous place and was curious about it.

We reached after half an hour. As I entered the market, I was shocked to see so many shops in a lane and everyone was selling clothes for women.

"Now, your time starts. Just walk with me. If you like anything just let me know."

I started looking. There were so many varieties of clothes and I was getting confused. I spent more than one hour in the first shop but I didn't get anything.

"What happened? You didn't like anything?"

"I'm very confused. There are so many shops with so many varieties of clothes and I do not know what to buy."

"Oh! You should have said something earlier. I told you I'm here to help you whenever you need it. I'll help you in deciding."

"Thank you so much."

"Okay, let's go to this shop," she said pointing at a shop.

We went to the shop and asked for jeans and tops. The shopkeeper showed us many pieces, but each time Aunty said no.

"Bhaiya, do you have any good piece in your shop?" she asked.

"Yes ma'am, I have."

"Well then show it to us fast. We're in a hurry"

"Ma'am, these two are the best pieces of our shop," he said as he showed us a really pretty outfit.

"Zeenat beti, do you like them?"

"Yes, aunty. They are very beautiful. I like them very much."

"How much are they for?"

"The jeans are for Rs. 1150 and the top for Rs. 850."

Fatima Aunty started bargaining in a way that I was shocked. He gave us both the things in just 1400 rupees.

We hired an auto rickshaw and headed back home.

"I was shocked to see you bargaining in this way with that shopkeeper."

"I'm fond of these all things. That was not new to me."

"You're truly an amazing person."

"Hahaha, no it is not like that. In these types of places, especially in Sarojini Market, they will tell you the double price of the product and at last, after bargaining, they will sell it for a good price."

"Hahaha, that's good to know."

"So, how was your shopping experience?"

"It was amazing. I bought clothes and also learnt many new things from you which are important for me."

"You're a good learner."

"One should always listen to other people. We should be a good listener and learner."

"You are right my dear daughter."

"Bhaiya stop here," I told the driver as soon I realized we had reached home.

"We were so busy in our chit- chat that we didn't even know how we reached home," I said.

"Yes, my dear but this is a good sign of our relationship. Isn't it?"

"Yes, it is and I'm very happy."

We entered the house and noticed that the door was open.

• • •

"Shoaib, Shoaib," aunty shouted as she entered.

Nobody was there. She sat on the sofa. I went to the kitchen and brought a glass of water for her.

"Fatima aunty please have a glass of water. Don't take stress," I offered her the glass.

"I'm not taking stress Zeenat but every day he does these types of silly things. He is not a child. He should understand this."

"Can I tell you one thing?" I asked.

"Yes, tell me," she replied.

"I'm not saying you are wrong. I'm just saying that uncle and you both should talk to him and I'm sure he'll understand."

"Perhaps you're right. I also hope he understands things soon."

"Sorry Zeenat, I forgot to ask you about food. I know you must be hungry."

"No, I'm not hungry, just a bit tired." "Okay, fine. You go to your room, freshen up and take some rest."

I went to my room. I waited for Umar uncle as I wanted to talk to him regarding my work in Benz cafe.

Fatima aunty came to my room.

"Zeenat, you were feeling tired so I brought you this fruit salad. Have it you'll feel refreshed."

"Thank you so much, Aunty."

"No need of thanks. Take rest. I'll leave now."

I woke up. I saw that the time was around 8:3. I didn't even remember when I fell asleep

As I went down from the stairs I saw Umar uncle talking on the phone and Fatima aunty cooking food in the kitchen.

He saw me.

"Zeenat beti, where are you going? Come here."

"Yes, I'm coming Umar uncle."

"So, how was your day?"

"It was very good. I enjoyed a lot."

"I heard that you and your aunt went shopping to Sarojini Market. How was it?"

"It was a good experience. I bought so many clothes for myself and even I learned many things from Fatima aunty."

"Zeenat, you wanted to talk to your uncle, tell him what you wanted to discuss," Fatima Aunty said as she entered the room.

"Yes, yes," I said.

"What happened Zeenat? Anything serious?" he asked.

"No, nothing serious. I just want to ask that, can I work at Benz Cafe? I really want to work there."

"Sure, but right now, it is not possible because there is no vacancy," he answered.

"Ok," I said.

"Tell me one thing, why do you want to work there?"

"I like the environment of Benz cafe and more importantly, I feel I will be able to handle it as the core task is hospitality and I love to serve people. That's why I am saying that I want to work there, but if it is not possible right now then okay but if there will be any vacancy then please take me into consideration."

"I'm really happy with your genuine answer. You have the same qualities like Rajiya had. Well, maybe at the end of this month, two people will leave their job, and then you can replace them."

"Okay, fine and thanks again."

"Welcome beti."

"I want to tell you one more thing, Uncle."

"Yes sure, say it without any hesitation."

"Actually, today morning I was helping Fatima aunty in the kitchen and she told me that I have to take your permission if I want to help her in the kitchen."

"See, beti you are very young. This is not the right time to get involved in kitchen activities. You should enjoy these days."

"I know you both love me, care for me, but I really want to help Fatima aunty because I love to work in the kitchen. I love to cook food for other people."

"Ok, if you really want to help her you can, but only once in a day."

"Thank you, uncle."

"Are you both not feeling hungry?" Aunty asked.

"Yes, we are," I said.

"Okay, then let's go to the dinner table."

Uncle and I were sitting on the chairs and waiting for food. Aunty came with Rajma, Rice, Shahi Paneer, Raita, and Papad.

"Today, you have cooked so many things. Is there anything special?" I asked.

"No beti. Every day we cook food like this."

"Okay but this all looks very delicious."

"In ashram, we never had so many varieties. We had the same menu for the entire year."

"Now this is your home. If you want to eat anything else just let me know I'll cook for you."

***

We finished the food while talking. Whenever I sat with them I always enjoyed, good things were entering my life and I was really happy. I also wished that someone would leave the job so that I can start work. I was eagerly waiting to meet Rajveer now.

"Zeenat, I wanted to talk to you about Rajiya and Dheeraj but right now I'm feeling really sleepy so I'll talk to you tomorrow."

"Ok, Goodnight Umar uncle."

"Zeenat, aren't you going to sleep?" Aunty asked.

"No, I already slept so much. I woke up just a few hours ago. So, now I'm not feeling sleepy."

"Okay then sit here, I'll come with my food."

"Wait, you are doing so much work from the morning. You sit here, I'll serve you food."

"No dear and it is not like that. This is my work, I have to do this."

"I agree with you. I'm not saying that you shouldn't do your work, but you should rest too, otherwise, it'll affect your health."

"You're absolutely right but sometimes we don't get time for ourselves.

"I know Fatima aunty, but you need to take time out for yourself." "I cannot win with you. From tomorrow I'll take care of myself."

"Hahaha, this is good." I laughed.

"I'm feeling very hungry. When will you give me food?"

"Oh! I am so sorry. I'm going."

I served the food to her and hugged her.

"Why are you crying Fatima aunty? You're like my mother."

"Nothing beti. Your presence reminds me of few mistakes that we did many years ago."

"What mistakes?

"I cannot tell you, sorry beti. We both had made a very big mistake that even God cannot forgive us."

"You both are very good. I don't believe this; the circumstances must be such that forced you to commit some mistake."

"I don't know beti but now we regret that mistake."

"I don't know anything but one thing I know you both cannot do anything wrong with anyone."

"Leave it beti. I'm feeling tired. I'm going to sleep now. Good night."

"Okay Aunty, we'll talk tomorrow. Good night."

I went to my room and was lying on the bed and thinking about Fatima aunty. Soon I fell asleep. My alarm clock rang at 5 in the morning. I opened my eyes. Still, that thing was going on in my mind. I refreshed myself. I was coming down from the stairs and saw Fatima aunty sitting alone on the balcony.

"What happened aunty, why are you sitting here?"

"Nothing beti. I was not feeling good. So, I thought of sitting alone, that's why I came here."

"Okay. Can I also sit here?"

"Yes beti. This is your home. You can sit anywhere. But why did you wake up so early?" she asked.

"I don't know my alarm rang so I woke up."

"Fatima aunty, can I say something?" I asked.

"Yes beti tell me."

"Don't feel guilty for your past mistakes because at times situations do not support us and we are forced to choose certain paths which ultimately leave us with regrets and sorrows."

"You talk like a mature person."

"Life has taught me a lot, aunty. I have faced so many things that now if something wrong happens, it seems trivial to me."

• • •

Part-2

I don't know what happened to you, but, I definitely want to know. I know I cannot lessen your pain or bring back whatever you have lost but I want you to share your sorrows with me as it might make you feel a little better."

"Yes, Fatima aunty you're right. We cannot change anything that has happened but we can share our sorrows with each other."

"Oh! We're late. We have been talking for last one hour. I'm going to the kitchen, after thirty minutes your uncle will ask for tea. He needs tea on his table at sharp 7 a.m."

"Ok, I'll come with you. Today, I'll make tea for Umar uncle."

We went to the kitchen and started preparing breakfast. I was enjoying my life with them. I made strong tea for Umar uncle, just the way he liked.

"Fatima aunty, I am going to serve uncle his tea."

I went to Umar uncle's room and knocked the door.

"May I come in?"

"Who's there?"

"Umar uncle, it's me, Zeenat."

I entered the room and kept his cup on the table that was right in front of him.

"Here's your tea. I have made it for you. Please let me know how is it?"

Umar uncle took the first sip of tea and I was eagerly looking at his expression.

"Beti, come here."

He opened his wallet and gave me five hundred and one rupees.

"The tea was very good. This is your reward for making something for the first time in our home. Take it, this is a tradition."

"Thank you, Umar uncle."

He put his hands on my head.

"God bless you, Beti."

"You both are very sweet. Amma told me so much about you, but you are a much more amazing person than those stories. I'm lucky that I got to start a new phase of my life with you guys."

"Hahaha…Thank you beti, even we are very lucky to get a daughter like you."

"I'll now go to the kitchen to help aunty with the breakfast."

I took the teacup and started walking towards the kitchen. I saw Fatima aunty was unconscious on the kitchen floor. I rushed to her.

"Fatima aunty! Fatima aunty?" I shook her, hoping she would wake up.

"Umar uncle, Umar uncle. Come fast, Fatima aunty has become unconscious."

Umar uncle rushed downstairs. He started shouting her name. I bought a glass of water and splashed a few drops on her face but she didn't move.

"Uncle, call the doctor."

Umar uncle ran towards his phone and started calling.

"He is coming within five minutes."

We took Fatima aunty toher room. I rubbed her feet with hot oil and within a few minutes, the doctor came. He started examining her.

Finally, Fatima aunty opened her eyes but she looked weak.

"I have given her a medicine. She is not serious, don't worry. She is taking a lot of stress these days and due to this her blood pressure got low," the doctor told us.

"Thank you, very much, doctor," Umar uncle said.

"Fatima don't take stress now."

"Yes, doctor."

"Zeenat, I'm coming in ten minutes. Take care of your aunty."

He went to escort the doctor out. I was looking into Fatima aunty's eyes.

"What is the time? Where is Shoaib? Has he not come home yet? Did anyone call him?" She asked.

"No, we didn't call him."

"Can you call him? I want to talk to him."

I dialed his number.

"His phone is switched off. Please don't be stressed, it is not good for your health. I will keep trying his number."

"Okay beti, whenever you talk to him just let me know."

"Sure aunty."

Generally, we don't respect those people who are always with us, who always stand with us in every problem. We are becoming selfish. We are forgetting our values and generosity.

I went out of the room. Umar uncle was sitting in the lobby area.

"What happened uncle?" I asked.

"Nothing beti, today is the last date of the month and one of the workers is leaving his job so I have to go to the café. But here your aunty is lying on the bed. How can I go?"

"You should go uncle and don't worry about her, I'm here. I'll take care of everything."

"But still beti, my heart is not allowing me to leave her in this condition."

"Then don't go for the whole day. You can go for two or three hours after that you come home."

"That's a good idea!"

"I'm going to the kitchen to prepare breakfast for you. You can go to your room and get ready."

"Okay beti. If you need anything from the kitchen just let me know."

"Sure uncle."

He went to the room and I started cooking. Within one hour, I have made paranthas for uncle and soup for aunty.

I went to their room. Umar uncle was sitting on the bed and Fatima aunty was sleeping.

"I have made breakfast. Should I serve it here only?"

"Yes, you can bring it here."

I went to the kitchen and brought breakfast for Umar uncle.

"I made cauliflower parantha and raita. I hope you like it."

"Of course. You are doing so much for us. We're very lucky to have you in our lives."

Umar uncle finished off the parathas within minutes. I was taking care of aunty.

"Beti, paranthas were really yummy. You even beat your aunty in cooking."

"Hahaha, she is like my mother and my master. I'm learning so many good things from her."

"That's good. Oh! Look at the time, I am so late. I'll leave now. Take care of your aunty and I'll be back in two hours."

"Okay Uncle, you need not worry I'll take good care of her," I said.

He left and I sat in Fatima aunty's room right beside her. I was feeling hungry so I went to the kitchen to eat something.

While I was having my breakfast, someone knocked the door. I went and opened the door, Shoaib was on the door.

"Where is mom?" he asked.

"She is in her room. Don't shout. She is sleeping; she fell unconscious because of low blood pressure. "

"Ok, I want to see her."

"You can see her; she is sleeping in her room. The doctor advised her to rest."

He went to Fatima aunty's room, looked at her and then went back to his room.

I started cleaning the house. Suddenly, I realized that uncle said that today one employee was leaving his job, it means from tomorrow I'll be working in Benz café! I was very happy. Now, I just had to wait for Umar uncle.

I heard Shoaib shouting my name.

"Zeenat, Zeenat, come here."

I went to his room.

"What happened, Shoaib?"

"Can you give me something to eat? I'm feeling very hungry."

"Yes, sure. Just wait for twenty minutes. I'll make your favourite fruit salad and shake."

"Oh! Thank you very much."

I went to Fatima aunty's room to check if she wanted something but she was still sleeping. So, I went to the kitchen and started cutting food and preparing shake for him.

"Shoaib, Shoaib," I called him.

"Yes?"

"I have made your salad and shake. Come here and take it."

As he was coming down the stairs, he was continuously looking at me.

He took everything and went to his room.

I cleaned the kitchen and then went to aunty. She was still sleeping. I was cleaning her room silently, thinking about tomorrow. Rajveer's face came in front of my eyes again and again. I even had to tell Umar uncle about Amma but everyday something or other happened. I decided that tonight, I'll definitely tell him everything.

"Zeenat, I'm going outside for some work. I'll be back in two hours. Please take care of mom," Shoaib said.

"Can I tell you something?" I asked.

"Yes, tell me."

"You're a very selfish person. Your mom is lying on the bed. She is ill you're leaving her. You should spend some time with her."

"Don't try to become my mother and lecture me."

"You get everything in your life easily that's why you don't care about anything. Just think about those people who have nothing in their life then you'll realize how lucky you are."

"I'm going, bye."

He went out of the room. Suddenly, Fatima aunty woke up.

"Where is Shoaib? Did he come?" she asked.

"Yes, he had come, but he went again for some work."

"I heard his voice. Were you both arguing?"

"No, we were not arguing. I was just telling him that he should spend some more time with you."

"Hmm… I need my son. He loves me very much but I don't know why he is behaving like this for the past few days."

"Aunty, I think you should talk to him personally, maybe he is in some kind of a problem these days and wants to talk to you."

"I think you're right. I'll talk to him soon."

"Sorry, I didn't ask you. How are you feeling now?"

"I'm feeling good now. You are doing so much for us. Thank you very much beti."

"On one side you're calling me beti and on the other side, you're saying thank you. Parents never say thanks to their children."

"Yes, you're right beti. I am sorry, no thank you."

I knew that when she wakes up, she would like to have masala tea.

"Aunty, I'm going to the kitchen. I have some work. I'll be back."

I went to the kitchen and started preparing masala tea for her. I saw Umar uncle entering the lobby.

"Zeenat how's your aunty now?" he asked.

"She is fit and fine, Uncle"

"What are you doing in the kitchen?"

"I'm making masala tea for her."

"Okay. I'm going to my room."

I made three glasses of tea. I went to their room and knocked the door.

"May I come in?" I asked.

"Come in beti. You don't need permission," Uncle replied.

"I have made masala tea for both of you."

"Oh! masala tea. We love masala tea."

"I know Umar uncle that's why I made it. I know whenever Fatima aunt wakes up from sleep, she needs one cup of masala tea and you also need it when you come from the café."

"Wow! You know so many things about us. You have done great research on us. Hahaha."

"Tell me. How's the tea?"

"I had tasted your tea before as well and I know everything you make is tasty. You're a perfect person. May God bless you with opulence and gaiety, beti."

"Thank you, uncle, for your wishes."

"Well, I have good news for you."

"What is it, uncle?"

"The good news is that you can join Benz Cafe from tomorrow."

"Seriously?"

"Yes beti. You can join from tomorrow and I'll be there to help you."

"I don't know what to say, this news has made my day. Thank you for everything."

"No need of thanks. I haven't done anything special for you. He left the job and you needed a job that's why you will be replacing him."

Umar uncle didn't know that he had helped me big time by giving me an opportunity to work there because now I could prove myself. Now, I was just waiting for tomorrow when I would work there and also I could talk to Rajveer.

"Umar uncle, I want to tell you something about Amma. You have asked me so many times. So, I thought I should tell you now."

"Yes, tell me beti."

"You both know that she is no more, that she had died in an accident but the truth is something else. Nobody knows the real truth," I said.

"What?" Aunty was shocked to hear this.

"Yes dear, she had mentioned about her death earlier. But I thought I would tell you after knowing the complete truth."

"What is the truth? Tell us now."

"The truth is she was murdered by Dheeraj. He murdered Amma."

"What are you saying? Do you have any idea? He was very close to her."

"Yes, I know but this is the reality. I tried to collect some proof against him but I failed. Even he tried to kill me but I ran away."

"Why are you telling everything so briefly? I want to know everything. Tell me," uncle urged.

"Ok Uncle, I'll tell you everything. Do you remember those days when Amma came to Delhi for work?"

"Yes, I do remember."

"It all started then. From the very beginning, when Dheeraj entered the ashram, he tried to touch me and get close to me but I ignored it because of Amma. But when Amma went to Delhi, he started coming regularly to my room and touched me without my permission. I told him many times that I will complain about him but day by day his courage increased.

One fine day, he came to my room, pushed me on the bed and started touching my private parts. I was helpless and could do nothing but cry. He raped me. He killed my soul. For the next few days, I locked myself in my room. I tried to commit suicide various times, but each time I stopped myself as Amma's face came in front of my eyes. I complained about him but nobody trusted me. They laughed at me. I realized that nobody is going to listen to me. Then he started coming every day to my room and assaulted me. I made one mistake, I told him I would complain to Amma and this was the reason he killed Amma. Actually, he hired a person who killed Amma. He is a murderer. He knew if I complain to Amma, he would be punished because she trusts me a lot. He even tried to kill me, but I escaped from that place. He is using Ashram's money for his personal benefit. I want to go back, but not now. I'll go there when I'll become independent, that's why I was asking for a job. So this is the whole story. "

"I don't believe this; you have faced so much at such a small age. You're a real fighter, my dear."

"Now, I just want to become a successful person so that I can take revenge and this is the only dream of my life, but first I want to focus on my career."

"We both will help you achieve your dreams. Don't worry. We're with you."

"Thank you, uncle. I had lost all hopes but then I met you both."

• • •

Part-3

"We always wished for a daughter like you, but we made a big mistake, that's why God never fulfilled our wish. Then we met you and you completed our wish. You're our daughter. Don't think that you have no one in your life. We're with you."

"A few days ago, Fatima aunty was also saying that you both have made a mistake, now again you're saying the same thing. You both are guilty of something and if you'll not share what is it, then for your whole life you'll regret it. You both can share this with me. Well, maybe I have no right to say anything to you because I'm not your real daughter, that's why you both are not saying anything."

"No, this is not true beti. Fine, I'll tell you," said Aunty. "Before Shoaib's birth, I was pregnant. We were very poor and that's why we had wished for a son. We decided to check the gender of the child. It is a crime, but we did it as we felt helpless. The doctor told us that the child is a daughter. We were facing a lot of financial problems at that time; we had no money for food. So, we took the sinful decision of killing our first child. We aborted the baby. Since then we regret our actions every single day of our life."

Aunty was almost in tears while narrating this incident.

"Sometimes, we have to bow down in front of situations. We need to work according to them. I know you regret your decision and feel guilty about it but time heals everything. One thing that I know is you both are very good from the heart," I tried to make Aunty feel better.

"Beti, you always motivate us. Well, leave all this now."

"Ok Aunty, now you take rest. I'll make dinner for everyone."

"No beti, you are doing ample of things since morning. Now, no need to work more. Sit here."

"No, Fatima aunty. You're not totally ok yet. Take rest. You can work from tomorrow."

"Ok Zeenat but no need to make too many dishes."

"Ok, Aunty."

I went to the kitchen. While cooking, many thoughts were running through my mind. My only aim in life is to take revenge on Dheeraj who destroyed everything in my life. He made my life hell and I knew Uncle-Aunty will help me become a successful person and support me in my aim. But on the other hand, Rajveer was distracting me from my aim. Every time his face came in front of my eyes, I had these thoughts. Just then, uncle entered the kitchen.

"Zeenat, I have called a tailor. When she comes, you give your measurements to her. She will make the uniform for you."

"Uniform for what Uncle?"

"You will be joining Benz cafe from tomorrow so would need a uniform."

"Oh, ok Uncle."

Uncle went back to his room and I resumed my cooking. After few minutes, I saw one lady entering the lobby area.

"Who are you? What do you want?" I asked.

"My name is Shabnam; Umar uncle called me and told me that I have to take someone's measurement for the uniform that's why I have come here," she replied.

"Okay. Yes, he told me. Sorry, I forgot. Can you wait for ten minutes? I'm cooking food."

"Yes, sure."

A few minutes later, I went to the lobby area where she was waiting for me.

"You can take my measurements for the uniform, I'm ready."

She came towards me, with the measuring tape and a notebook and started measuring me.

"We are done," she said after noting all of my measurements.

"Thank you for coming. When will you deliver the dress?"

"You'll get it within two days."

"Okay, thank you very much."

"My pleasure, ma'am."

I went back to the kitchen and started making rice and chapati for everyone.

"Zeenat, did the tailor come?" Uncle asked when he came down.

"Yes, she came and I have given my measurements."

"Oh! That's great. Did she mention when the uniform will be ready?"

"Within two days."

"Great! You can come in casuals till you get it."

"Ok Uncle."

I made dinner and then went back to my room. I was feeling tired, so I went to bed and tried going to sleep.

After two hours I woke up and looked at the clock, it was 8:20. I washed my face and went to Fatima aunty's room. I saw they were both sleeping so I didn't disturb them. I went back to my room and started ironing my clothes for tomorrow. Then after a few minutes, I heard Umar uncle's voice.

"Zeenat beti, what are you doing? Come here."

I went to their room and knocked on the door.

"May I come in?" I asked.

"Yes, come in," he instantly replied.

"Uncle, you called me?" I said.

"Yes, but Zeenat, I have told you many times to not knock on this door. No need to take permission."

"Sorry. I will take care from next time."

"Good. We both are really hungry and your aunt is also getting late for her medicines which she has to take after dinner."

"Alright. The dinner is ready; I'll just heat the dal and sabzi. You both come to the table while I do that."

"That's great! We'll be there in ten minutes."

I went to the kitchen after a few minutes uncle aunty came as well.

"I have made Rice, Dal, Chapatis, Paneer ki sabzi and Papad for everyone," I said as I placed everything on the table.

They started eating and I sat there to serve them. "Zeenat, you have cooked delicious food. You break all of your aunty's records. You're really an amazing person. You're perfect in everything."

"No one is perfect Uncle. I'm just doing those things which I like the most and know how to do."

"Zeenat, you're an example of the best daughter. I don't why God has taken your test so many times but I know that good days are waiting for you. Soon, they will enter your life," Aunty said.

"Thanks for believing in me and thanks for understanding me every time, Aunty."

• • •

"We should also be thankful to you because you understand us very well. You're the one with whom we share our mistakes and our regrets."

"I know and I feel very lucky."

"Zeenat, you should also have your dinner. It's 9:20 p.m., you're getting late. You will have to come with me to the café tomorrow."

"Yes, uncle. I'll just have it after cleaning up. Don't worry, I'll be ready tomorrow."

"Great beti. So, we are going to our room because I'm feeling tired and she also needs to rest."

"Ok uncle, if you need anything, just call me."

"Ok. Good night Zeenat."

"Good night Uncle-Aunty."

I cleaned the dining table and start eating dinner. I was really hungry, but I stopped myself as I did not feel comfortable to ask for second helpings. I finished my dinner within ten minutes; after that, I started cleaning all utensils. After wrapping up, I finally switched off all the lights and went back to my room. I had to wake up early the next day so, I went to bed and closed my eyes.

I don't remember when I slept. Actually, I was feeling tired. Next day in the early morning, my alarm rang and I woke up. I freshened up in half an hour and went to the kitchen. Fatima aunty was there.

"What are you doing here?" I asked.

"Nothing Zeenat. Today is your first day on the job so I'm doing everything for you."

"But you're not well. You need bed rest."

"No, I'm totally fine. I don't need any bed rest. You don't worry."

"Okay Aunty, but don't over-stress yourself."

"Ok. What are you doing here?"

"I came here to make breakfast. But you're doing everything and I know you'll not allow me to help you. So, I think I should go from here."

"Yes, I'm not going to allow you. Go to your room, take rest and be ready for your first day at the job."

"Ok I'm going but if you need any help, call me please."

"Yes, sure Zeenat. Don't worry."

I went back to my room and started getting ready. I was very happy because I was going to meet Rajveer and that it was the first day of my job. I wore black jeans and a white shirt. I got ready within forty minutes and went back to the kitchen.

"How am I looking?" I asked.

"Wow! Beautiful. You're looking gorgeous in that black and white combination," Aunty replied with a smile.

"Seriously?"

"Yes, Zeenat beti seriously. You can ask your uncle. Come with me."

We went to uncle's room. He was reading a newspaper.

"How am I looking Umar uncle?"

"You're looking very beautiful my daughter," he said after looking at me carefully.

"Thanks to both of you for motivating me. You both have made my life beautiful."

"Zeenat beti, you have also made our life beautiful. You completed our wish. You brought happiness to our life. We don't need anything more from life. Now, I'll also go and get ready, give me half an hour."

• • •

"Okay, Umar uncle."

I went to my room and kept looking at myself in the mirror again and again. That was the first time; I was admiring myself.

"Zeenat, come here. Your breakfast is ready."

"Coming!"

I kept everything in my bag, closed my room's door and went to the kitchen.

"Zeenat, this is your masala tea and paranthas. Have it."

"Thank you so much, aunty."

I was eating paranthas when Umar uncle also came there.

"Fatima, give me my breakfast. I'm getting late."

"Yes, here is your breakfast."

"Zeenat, hurry up. We have to leave before 9 a.m."

"Yes uncle, I'm almost done."

After a few minutes, I had finished my food and went to the kitchen. I placed the utensils and washed my hands.

I touched Fatima aunty's feet and took her blessings.

"God bless you beti."

Umar uncle and I left home. We were going in the car and I was very excited about everything. We reached at 9:25 a.m. and I opened the car door to step out.

"Zeenat, I'm coming, you go ahead and introduce yourself to everyone."

"Ok, Sir," I teased him.

Benz Cafe

I entered the café through the front door. Everyone looked up, especially Ajay sir.

"Welcome, Zeenat, to the Benz family," Ajay said with a clearly fake smile.

"Thank you, Ajay Sir."

I was introducing myself to everyone when Umar uncle entered.

"Ajay, she is the new employee of Benz Cafe. So, introduce yourself to each other and then report to my office in fifteen minutes."

"Okay Sir," Ajay said.

For the first time I saw Umar Uncle like this, but I knew this was because Uncle kept personal and professional life separate. He handles both the things very well. I continued introducing myself to others.

"I think we should report to Umar sir. He is waiting for us," Ajay said.

"Yeah ok, let's go."

We went to Umar uncle's office and everyone was tensed as he had called an urgent meeting. Ajay knocked the door.

"May I come in, Sir?" Ajay asked.

"Yes, come in Ajay." He replied.

"Ajay, Zeenat is new here. You'll teach her everything. You're the most trusted person here, and I know you'll do this work honestly. Rest everyone will help you and I hope everyone will maintain peace of this café."

"Yes sir," Ajay said.

We went to our respective places we started doing our work. After some time, Ajay came to me.

"Are you feeling good here, Zeenat?"

"Yes, I'm good, Thank you."

"Okay, if you need any help then you can tell me. I know you're very close to Umar sir."

"Okay, Ajay sir."

As we were talking, I saw Rajveer entering the cafe.

"Ajay, give me one Cappuccino," Rajveer said.

"Yes sir, just give me five minutes."

Ajay sir made cappuccino for him. I wanted to take the order to him.

"Ajay sir, Can I take this order?" I asked.

"Yes but make sure that everything should be done correctly because he is our regular customer."

"Okay sir, don't worry I'll not disappoint you."

I took the cappuccino and went towards Rajveer's seat. He was busy fiddling with his mobile."Sir, here is your order, one hot cappuccino."

"Thank you, ma'am," he said without looking up.

"Welcome, sir."

I was going back when he suddenly called my name.

"Zeenat, do you work here now?"

"Yes, I have started working here from today."

He nodded. I headed back to my work and resumed my job. Customers were coming and going and we were all doing our jobs. He came near the cash counter and sat there.

"Ajay, give me one more cappuccino."

"Yes sir, your order coming right up," Ajay sir said instantly.

After five minutes, Ajay sir called me. "Zeenat please take this order to Rajveer sir."

"Yes, sir."

I took the order and went to him.

"Sir, here is your one hot cappuccino."

"Thank you, ma'am," this time he looked up and smiled.

When I was serving him, I saw Shanaya entering the cafe with her rich friend, Rahul.

"How are you, Ajay?" She asked.

"I am good, ma'am."

"Rajveer darling, how are you?"

"I'm fine baby," he said as he hugged her.

"Sorry for being late. I was stuck in traffic."

"It is ok, Shanaya."

"Excuse me, ma'am?" he called me.

"Yes, sir. How can I help you?" I asked.

"Kindly get us two more cappuccinos."

"Okay Sir, anything else?"

"No, that's it."

"You, beggar! What are you doing here?" Shanaya shouted at me with anger.

"Sorry ma'am, my name is Zeenat and I'm not a beggar. I work here," I said with a smile.

"No, you're a beggar."

"Sorry ma'am, I have to leave, I have to take other orders too."

I left in a huff. I could see that she was mortified by me, Rajveer was trying to placate her and make her understand.

"What happened Zeenat? Is everything fine?" Ajay asked.

"Yes, everything is fine. Don't worry sir."

After few hours, Ajay came to me.

"Zeenat, this is lunch time. Go and have some food."

"I have to finish this work, I'll go after that."

I was wrapping up my work when Umar uncle stopped by.

"Zeenat, did you eat something?"

"No, sir, not yet."

"Okay then come with me. I'm going for lunch."

"No, sir. It's okay," I instantly replied feeling embarrassed by this special treatment.

"Zeenat, come with me. I know you're hungry."

"Okay, sir. I'm coming."

Other than Ajay sir, nobody knew that I was living in Umar uncle's house so everyone stared at me when I was going with him for lunch. We went to a nearby restaurant where Umar uncle usually went for lunch.

"I like your behavior in the cafe. You know how to balance your personal and professional life."

"Yes, beti. If you know how to handle both things, then you'll never face problems."

"You're truly right."

"I'm feeling very hungry. I'm going to place my order, what do you want to have?

"I don't want to eat anything special, Uncle. I'll share your order only."

"Waiter, come here!" he called.

"Yes, sir. What can I get you?"

"One dal, Shahi Paneer, rice, and six chapatis."

"I'll get your order in fifteen minutes."

"Okay, dear."

After a few minutes, the waiter came with our order and we started eating. I was enjoying the new journey of life. Everything was going well.

"Are you enjoying your work?"

"Yes uncle, I am loving it."

"When you were serving coffee to Rajveer, I heard some commotion. I think Shanaya was shouting at you. Is everything alright?"

"Yes, everything is alright, you don't need to worry."

"They are the children of rich people and our regular customers. They are very egoistic thanks to their parent's money. Out of all of them, Rajveer is the only one who is humble and kind. He respects other people and everyone likes him."

"Yes, he is different from his friends. I didn't tell you one thing. When I came to the café for the first time, Shanaya insulted me, but he was the one who came and fought with his own friends. He even gave me money for food."

"This is totally wrong. Why didn't you tell me earlier? Why are you telling this now?" he asked angrily.

"I didn't think it was a big issue so I didn't say anything before."

"Fine, but from now onwards, no need to hide anything from me. I'm your boss in the office not at home."

"Okay, uncle."

We finished our lunch and then went back to the cafe.

• • •

I entered the cafe and saw Rajveer sitting alone at the same table. It seemed like he was waiting for someone. We had an eye contact. His eyes were trying to say something but I was helpless as there were many people.

"Zeenat, can you please get me a glass of water?" he asked.

"Sure sir!" I replied.

I went to his table

"Sir, your water."

"Thanks, Zeenat and sorry for what happened this morning. Shanaya is a nice girl but is short tempered."

"Sir, please don't say sorry. She is our customer and for me, our customers are equal to God."

"You're so sweet, dear. I mean she insulted you twice but still, you have nothing bad in your heart for her."

"Sir, we are poor people. All we expect is three meals a day. We have no time to hate anyone."

"A person is rich in real sense when he/she has the courage to forgive other people when he/she accepts the other person despite their caste, creed, or color and you're one of them. So, don't say that you're poor. You are rich from the heart."

"Sir, I don't know these things, but you're a very good human being. You helped me that day also."

"Thank you, Zeenat."

"Zeenat, come here," Ajay sir called.

"Yes, sir. I'm coming."

I went back. I started my work again. I was learning how to make different products of Benz café. It was an amazing experience. Everyone was being very cooperative with me.

"Today, Rajveer has been sitting here for a really long time. His friends have gone, but he is still here. He even ordered six coffees. I am unable to understand this change; do you know anything about it?" Ajay said.

"I also don't know anything, sir."

I had decided to just ignore him, but he was continuously looking at me. I kept pretending to be busy.

"Ajay, can you get me the bill?" he said.

"Yes, sir. Just two minutes."

Ajay sir gave him the bill. He made the payment and left the place. While going out from the cafe, he kept looking at me. I was unable to understand what he wanted.

"Zeenat, I'm watching both of you since morning. He has been continuously staring at you and you both were talking to each other for a really long time. Is anything wrong?" Sonia, who was another employee, asked me.

"No, nothing is wrong. Don't worry. He helped me on my first day and I was just thanking him."

"Okay."

The was a shift for female employees was from 9:00 a.m. to 5:00 p.m. So, the three of us were finishing our work, when Umar uncle came.

"Zeenat, you'll go back with me."

"No Uncle, I'll leave. You don't worry."

"No, I said you'll go with me."

"Sir, I have some work at home. That's why I have to go. I'll be careful, I promise."

"Okay, but take care of yourself."

"Yes, sir, " I said.

I finished my work and started packing my bag.

"I'm leaving. Goodbye Ajay Sir."

"Goodbye, Zeenat."

I came out of the cafe and hired an auto from Benz cafe for home. Fatima aunty had said that Delhi is not safe for girls at night. But I was afraid of nothing as I had already faced the worst situations in my life. After twenty-five minutes, I reached home.

I entered the house and saw Fatima aunty sitting in the lobby area and doing some work.

"How was your day my daughter?" she asked.

"I learned few new things there. The overall experience was good, Aunty."

"Good. Go, freshen up and take rest."

"Yes, I'm going. I'm feeling a little bit tired."

"Fine. I'll bring your masala tea to your room. It will remove all your stress."

"Hahaha okay. Thank you."

I went to my room. I was really very tired. I got refreshed and then without wasting any time I went to bed and closed my eyes.

"Zeenat, Zeenat wake up."

I awoke listening to Aunty's voice.

"What happened Fatima aunty?"

"Come and have dinner, beti. You have been sleeping for almost four hours. It's 9:30 p.m."

"Shit! Sorry. I just closed my eyes. I don't know when I fell asleep. Just give me five minutes, I'm coming."

"Okay, but come fast. Your uncle is waiting on the dinner table."

I washed my face and then went to lobby area.

"Thank you, Umar uncle for supporting me."

"What happened?"

"Nothing much."

"Ok, I'm feeling hungry today."

"Same here."

"Actually, we had lunch around 2:00 p.m. and now it's 9:30 p.m. This gap of seven hours is why we are feeling hungry."

"Yes, you're right Uncle."

"Fatima come fast."

"I'm coming. Give me two minutes."

After a few minutes, Fatima aunty came to dinner. She gave us plates and served the food. We started our dinner. As I was eating, I thought about different phases of my life. It was a soul breaking experience. I also thought the reason why Rajveer was staring at me continuously in the café. I figured I should talk to Fatima aunty when Umar uncle goes to his room after dinner.

"Zeenat, what happened? Why are you so quiet today? Is everything okay?" he asked.

"Yes, everything is fine."

We finished our dinner and Uncle went to his room. I was sitting in the lobby area waiting for Fatima aunty after keeping our dishes in the kitchen."Fatima aunt, please sit here. I'll serve you dinner now."

"Okay beti."

I brought and served her food, she started eating.

"Fatima aunty, I want to ask you something."

"Yes, tell me."

"Actually, when the first time I went to the cafe, I met a guy named Rajveer. He helped me a lot; he even fought with his friends for me. But he was staring at me continuously that day and the same thing happened today also. His face is, again and again coming in front of my eyes."

"Zeenat, beti, this is the age where we take so much stress on these things. You're thinking too much. Maybe he is a good person by heart that's why he helped you. There can be ‘n' number of reasons. We cannot conclude anything on the basis of one or two days' happenings. Don't worry. Everything will be fine."

"Yes, you're right. I'm thinking too much. I'll ignore him from tomorrow."

"Have you made any mistake?"

"No."

“So, why will you ignore him? Don't make this mistake. Just do your work there and enjoy life. Don't take stress."

"Ok aunty, I'll follow your advice."

"Now, go to your room and sleep."

"Yes, I'm going. Thank you for your advice."

"You are welcome, my dear. I'm always with you. Don't worry."

"Bye. Good night, Aunty"

"Bye. Good night. Take care."

I went back to my room. I thought maybe Fatima aunty was right. I was thinking too much about him.

The next day in the early morning, my alarm rang. I woke up with its voice. I freshened up and went to the kitchen and helped Aunty for breakfast. It was my duty. I was living in their house; they did not ask me for any money. They have done so much for me and were still doing. They treat me like their own daughter. So, it was my responsibility to help them in all possible ways.

• • •

We are human beings. We shouldn't forget our moral values because it teaches us so many things at each point in life.

"You're a very responsible person. You will definitely achieve heights of opulence, more importantly, you know the difference between good and bad," Aunty said.

"Thank you, Fatima aunty. I learned so much from you and I want to learn more because I think we should always learn from others."

"Yes, we should always learn something from others as we are all learners."

"I'm going to my room to get ready."

"Okay, beti."

I took a cup of tea and went to my room. I started ironing my clothes. I got ready within half an hour. Like yesterday, I went to the lobby area for breakfast. Umar uncle was sitting there.

"Good morning, Zeenat beti."

"Good morning, Umar uncle."

"So, are you ready for today?"

"Yes, I'm. I am enjoying my job."

"Fatima, how much time will you take for breakfast?"

"Just give me ten minutes. I'm coming."

After a few minutes, she came to the dining table and served us the breakfast. We ate and headed to the cafe.

I was sitting in the car and Umar uncle drove.

The moment I entered the café, I saw Rajveer sitting there already. His eyes looked like he was waiting for someone.

"Good Morning, Ajay Sir."

"Good Morning, Zeenat."

Umar uncle entered the cafe and we were supposed to report to his office for a morning meeting.

"Your lover was waiting for you, go and meet him," Sonia said.

"What are you saying? I do not understand," I replied.

"Yes, he is your lover. He came here when Ajay sir was just opening the café."

"He is not my lover. I don't know him personally and stop saying these rubbish things."

"Zeenat, Sonia, come with me. We have to report to Umar Sir's office," Ajay sir called us.

We went to Umar uncle's office.

"So, guys, how's the work going? Is everything fine?" he asked.

"Yes, everything is fine sir," Ajay sir replied, "Zeenat has learned many new things. She has especially learnt how to make perfect cups of cappuccinos."

"That's great. From now on, she will also help you in making other products."

"Okay, sir."

"Good. Go and start your work. Customers are waiting to order."

We went back to work.

"Ajay, give me one cappuccino," Rajveer ordered.

"Yes sir," Ajay sir replied.

I started making cappuccino for him. I took the order and asked Sonia to wait on his table. He was sitting just in front of the cash counter so, I was clearly able to see him and listen to their conversation as well.

"He has been asking for you," Sonia said.

"Seriously?"

"Yes."

"Leave it. I don't know what he wants."

"Well…everyone has been talking about you and Rajveer."

"Ok, but I don't care because I know I'm right and not doing anything wrong."

"Okay. I was just letting you know."

"Thank you for your concern."

I felt that if Umar uncle gets to hear this from anyone else, he would be hurt. I wanted to tell him anything on my own; I wanted to tell him just as he had confided in me. I just had to wait for the right time.

As I was working, Umar Uncle came to me.

"Zeenat, Come here."

"Yes, sir," I instantly replied.

"Is everything good?"

"Everything is good. I just wanted to share one thing with you."

"Yes, tell me."

"I heard that everyone is spreading rumors that there is something happening between me and Rajveer but there's no such thing. We don't even know each other."

"I had heard this rumor, that's why I was asking you again and again if everything is ok but you didn't tell me. Anyway, don't worry; I trust you and I don't care about rumors."

"Thank you, Umar Sir. Thank you for believing in me."

"You are welcome, Zeenat. Now, let's get back to work."

"Yes, sure."

I went back to my work. I couldn’t help but notice his expression, he seemed disturbed. I saw Shanaya and Rahul walking in and start talking with him. The most annoying thing about Shanaya is that she is very loud.

"Rajveer darling, what are you doing here? We were calling you since last night. Everyone is worried about you."

"I just want to spend some time by myself. I don't need anyone. So, leave me alone and don't disturb me."

"We are your friends. We are worried about you. Please tell me what happened?"

"Shanaya, I said leave me alone why don't you understand?" he shouted.

"Fine. Do what you want to do. We will not ask you anything."

"Thank you very much, both of you," he said and went out of the cafe.

I could hear their conversation. Suddenly, she came towards me.

"You are the reason for everything. I'll see you. I'll never forgive you," she shouted angrily.

"What are you saying, ma'am? I don't know anything."

"Don't act like an innocent girl. We know everything about you."

"I don't know what you are talking about, so please ma'am, stop. Don't blame me for anything."

"You will pay for this. Remember, you have to pay," she shouted and went from the cafe.

"What happened Zeenat?" Ajay sir came to me after hearing her shout at me.

"I didn't do anything. Why was she overreacting?”

"Shanaya loves Rajveer. They are childhood friends, maybe that's why she was overreacting."

"I didn't do anything, sir, even I don't know him personally."

"I know Zeenat. Leave it. Let's head back to work."

"Thank you very much, sir."

We went back to work; she had disturbed the whole environment of the cafe but, I managed somehow.

Every day after that I had the same routine. From home to cafe, then cafe to home. Life was going on the right track and I was happy. I enjoyed with Fatima aunty and Umar uncle. However, from last couple of days, he had not come to the café and I was worried. I was unable to understand why I cared for him.

One day, when I was sitting in the garden area, Fatima aunty came.

"We have been watching you from last few days. Why do you make this sad face? It doesn't suit you. What happened? Is everything alright, beti?"

"I don't know, but I feel like I'm missing something."

"What are you missing? Tell me clearly."

Part-1

"Remember, I told you about Rajveer? I tried my best to ignore him but I failed. Now he is not coming to the cafe for last few days and my eyes are stuck at the cafe's gate waiting for him. I don't understand my behaviour at all."

"Oh! So this is the issue and here I was thinking something bad has happened. Well, don't worry, you're just attracted towards him and this is quite common for your age. Hadn't he helped you when everyone was against you? So obviously it enhances your feelings for him. That's why you want to see and talk to him."

"I don't know if you're right or wrong but I am desperate to talk to him. I cannot see myself like this."

"Don't worry, he might be busy that's why he is not coming. Wait for a few days more, he will definitely come and then you can talk to him."

"I think you're right. I'll wait for him."

"Good. Okay, now I'm leaving. I have some work."

Days went by and I kept waiting for him. Everything looked dull. Even Umar uncle and Fatima aunty asked me many times that why I was so sad. I also didn't know the reason; I don't think I will be able to find the reason until I meet him again. One fine day, Sonia was on leave and Ajay sir and Umar uncle had gone to a meeting. I was looking after everything: taking orders, making food, managing the cash, keeping things clean…let's just say it was a hectic day. I was taking payment from customers when suddenly I saw him coming towards the café. The moment I saw him, I smiled. I felt like I had found something that had gone missing.

"Yesterday, Rahul told me that Shanaya insulted you the other day. I really don't know what to say, but I'm really sorry for everything. Every time she insults you because of me and you never say anything to her. You're great. I'm feeling guilty for that day so, sorry again," he said to me.

"Where were you from the last few days? Why didn't you come here? I was worried about you. Why don't you understand such a simple thing?" I asked tears welled up in my eyes.

"Don't worry. I'm fit and fine. I was finding answers to some of my questions and now your tears have given me my answers."

"What are you saying?"

He held my shoulder, hugged me, and kissed my forehead."Nothing," he answered.

The moment he hugged and kissed me was one of the best moments of my life. My heartbeat increased. This was the first time I was feeling safe with someone, the first time I was notuncomfortable with someone's touch, the first time someone touched my soul and not my body. Everyone was watching us but I didn't care.

"Go and take your seat. I'll be back with your favorite cappuccino."

"Okay," he smiled.

This time his stare gave me happiness. I started making his coffee and I put my own touch on it.

"Rajveer, your cappuccino is ready!"

"Thanks, Zeenat."

I went back to the cash counter. We kept looking at each other. I made cappuccino and other drinks for customers. I put the burger in the oven for heating. He was distracting me, but I was happy with this distraction. As I was taking out the burger from the oven, my little finger touched the hot oven. The moment he saw my pain, he came to me.

"Are you mad? Where is the icebox?"

"Don't worry. Everything is fine."

"Nothing is fine."

He held my hand and put my fingers in the icebox. I could see pain reflected in his eyes. Even though the pain, everything seemed beautiful. I finally had someone whom I can trust. In last few months, he had become very close to me. Maybe, he was the person for me that's why day by day we were getting close. However, I did not trust my destiny. I didn't want to lose him because I had already lost my Amma who loved me.

"Rajveer, you should go. Everyone is looking at us."

"Okay. But promise me you'll take care of yourself because your life is not just your life now. You have become someone else's life too."

"Okay, I promise. I'll take care of myself."

He went to his table. Most of our conversations were going on with eyes now. Slowly everyone started leaving, it was around 5:45 p.m. We were still looking at each other. After everyone had left, he walked towards me."

"Rajveer, I don't know whether this is wrong or right but whenever I see you, a smile comes on my face. I feel safe with you."

"I know many girls. I talk to them, but all those girls only have a pretty face, they don't have their own minds. You're different from all of them. I like your thinking, your mindset. I like the essence of your soul."

This was enough for me. I had no words to say and had tears in my eyes. He held me in his arms and kissed my forehead. We were getting closer to each other. Suddenly the cafe's telephone started ringing.

"Wrong timing," he said with a smile.

I picked the call with a smile on my face, it was Umar uncle on-line. We had a conversation for a few minutes.

"Who was on the call?" he asked.

"Umar uncle was on the call. He said that he will not come so I have to close the cafe now."

"Okay, you close up. I'm waiting for you outside the café."

"Okay. I'm coming in ten minutes."

I closed the shop within a few minutes as I was in a hurry. First time in my life, I was going to be with the person who cared for me, loved me, respected me, and valued me more than anyone else.

We were going in the car. I was looking at him again and again. He was my stress buster. He was everything a girl could ever wish for in her life: tall, white with a muscular body, rich, and a pure heart always ready to help others. Life with him after so many bad times was like heaven. Few months were like few minutes and each minute felt like perpetuity. While driving the car he didn't speak anything but our hearts knew everything.

"I want to spend my whole life with you," he said.

"I also want to spend my whole life with you, but the reality is I am not the right one for you. I have a very bad past. I want to tell you many things, but this is not the right time."

"Everyone has a past and I don't care about your past. I want to make the best of our present and future."

"This society will never accept our relation. Your parents will never accept me. My aim of life is different and I have to complete that."

"Do you trust me?" He asked.

"Yes, I do."

"Then just trust me and please give me one chance. Don't spoil everything on the basis of your past."

"Okay. I need some time, but I'm not giving you any surety."

"That's fine. I know you and I trust your decisions."

"One more thing, we will not talk at the café as few people don't like it and I don't want to give chances to them. People are already talking about us and they are spreading rumors which I don't like. Umar uncle trusts me a lot. I don't want to break his trust. I'll tell him everything personally, but when the right time comes."

"Okay. I'll come to the cafe every day with my friends. We will not talk, happy?"

"Yes, now I am happy and I hope you understand."

"Yes, I understand, don't worry. I'm with you, Zeenat."

"Thank you."

"I accepted whatever you said but now you have to also accept one thing."

"What?"

"I'll not talk to you at the café, but I'll drop you home every day in the evening and you have to accept this. You have no other option."

"Okay."

"And one more thing, I want to celebrate my birthday with you, not just this year, every year. Maybe, I'm being selfish but I have realized that my happiness lies with you."

"Your birthday? Sure, I also want to celebrate your birthday. I have never celebrated anyone's birthday but I want to celebrate yours. So, don't worry I'll be there. But, I haven't told you anything about my life, Rajveer. I have faced so many things and when you will come to know about my past then definitely your thinking will change."

"I love you and this is enough for me to spend my whole life with you. I want to become your shadow and a shadow never leaves the person."

"You always make me speechless with your words. I am getting late. I have to go," I said.

"Okay. Bye. Take care."

"Bye. Take care."

When I got down from the car, I saw Shoaib watching me. He didn't say anything, but his eyes spoke a lot, the way he looked at me, I didn’t feel good.

I entered home and saw everyone was sitting in the lobby area, waiting for me.

"Sorry, Zeenat beti. I couldn't come to the cafe. I got so busy with work.”

"That is ok, Uncle. I handled everything. No doubt, it was a hectic day, but I enjoyed a lot."

"Good."

"I'm feeling tired now so, I'll head to my room."

"Okay beti go and take rest."

I went to my room and tried to sleep. But a lot of negative thoughts swam through my mind. I was scared because Shoaib has seen me get down from the car. I knew I was not doing anything wrong but if Umar uncle comes to know from some other person then definitely I'll lose everyone's trust. So, I decided that I'll tell everything to Umar uncle soon.

Next evening when I was taking orders from the customers, I saw Rajveer and his friends, Shanaya and Rahul, come towards the cafe.

"Excuse me, Ma'am," Rajveer said coming to the cash counter.

"Yes, sir. What can I get you?" I instantly asked.

"Three cappuccinos and three burgers."

"Anything else, Sir?"

"No, ma'am. How much do I have to pay?"

"Six hundred thirty-five rupees."

"Okay, ma'am."

"Thank you very much, sir. Have a nice day."

"You too, ma'am"

He made the payment and went back to his friends at their favorite table the first time, Shanaya was enjoying with everyone and more importantly, she didn't shout at anyone. I couldn't resist but smile at our conversation that just happened. He was doing just what I had asked him to and I was happy because no one was watching us.

"Zeenat, you're doing a good job. You forgot all the past things. You're very strong," Ajay sir said.

"Thank you very much, sir."

All day, I would keep waiting for the evenings when I could go and spend some time with him. I knew what I was doing was wrong, but everything seemed so right and so good. At sharp 5, I used to leave the cafe with him. We spent only twenty minutes with each other in a day, but those minutes were enough for both of us. Those minutes were enough to reduce my entire day's tiredness. He used to drop me just a few meters away from home.

One day, he dropped me and I was walking towards home when suddenly someone called my name. I turned back and was shocked to see Shoaib there.

"I'm watching you from last few months, you always come with that person."

"So what? Did you see anything wrong?"

"No, but I didn't tell this to anyone. And now, I'm thinking I should tell Mom and Dad."

"Okay, go and tell."

"Fine. Now, you just wait and watch."

I reached home after a few minutes and went straight to my room. I was lying on my bed, thinking about Shoaib's words. I was scared because I knew him. He hated me so much and I didn't even know the reason. I wanted to talk to them, but I was waiting for the right moment.

The next morning, as I was getting ready for the cafe, I heard Umar uncle's voice.

"Zeenat, Zeenat."

I came out from my room."Yes, Umar uncle. What happened?"

"Come here. I need to talk to you."

"I'm getting ready. I'll be there in ten minutes."

"No, you're not going to the cafe today. Come here."

I rushed downstairs as I could guess the anger in Uncle's voice... I saw Fatima aunty and Shoaib sitting there. Shoaib was talking to both of them and they were looking at some photographs.

"Why did you do this to us?" he asked.

"What happened, Umar uncle?"

"Look at these photographs, I told you before that if you have anything in your mind or heart, you can tell me."

I saw the photographs. In each photograph, I and Rajveer were very close. I looked at Fatima aunty's face. She was also helpless in front of everyone.

"Umar uncle, this is not the reality. Please try to understand me."

"Now, don't try to fool me again. We trusted you so much and this is what you did! You broke our trust."

"No, Please try to understand me. These photos are not showing the reality, these are deceptive," I said with tears in my eyes.

"We trusted you so much. We shared everything with you. We treated you as our daughter. At least you should have told us."

"Fatima aunty, please! I have told you everything. You know everything. Please say something, if you'll not say today, then it will create a big mess," I requested and tears rolled from my eyes.

"I don't know anything Zeenat. Don't ask anything from me."

I was helpless in front of everyone and Shoaib was proving me wrong. I had no way to prove myself. I requested, even begged many times, but nobody was listening to me.

"You are not going to the café from now on. You will stay at home."

"Please don't do this to me. I came here for work. Please!"

"You have broken our trust. Now, I can't trust you."

"You all have an issue with Rajveer. Fine, I'll not meet him, in fact, I'll not even see him from now, but please allow me to work at the café."

"Fine, but if I see you with him then I'll directly terminate you from the café."

•••

"Okay."

I had no other option. I couldn't sacrifice my aim for anyone. Moreover, I thought I'll make everyone understand slowly and steadily. I went back to my room and got ready and headed to café with Uncle. As Rajveer and I had already discussed that we'll not talk in the café, we followed the same. I knew Umar uncle was watching us.

"Are you not talking to Rajveer?" Sonia asked.

"No, I'm not. We have nothing going on. Everyone is just spreading rumors and I don't care about anyone."

I had decided that today would be the last day when I would talk to him. At sharp 5 I finished my work.

After a few minutes, his car came. He was smiling. He came out from the car and hugged me.

"Zeenat, sorry for today. I was very busy. Let's go. Don't waste time here."

I didn't say anything, neither did I move from my place. He understood everything.

"What happened?" he asked.

"Nothing. From today we will not meet. This is my final decision."

"What are you saying? What happened? Please tell me, Zeenat!"

"Please forget me. I said earlier that people will not accept our relation so please just leave me alone."

"And I also told you I don't care about society. Why are you not getting it?"

"But I do. I want to live here. I have nothing. I have few people in my life and I don't want to lose them at any cost."

"Don't do this to me. I cannot live with you."

"I understand but I have no other option because I already promised Umar uncle that we will never meet again."

"Fine. Don't worry. I'll not meet you again. I'll never see your face. But I want to tell you one thing, the last few months were the best months of my life. The roller coaster ride we had, the time we spent, the moments we created are the best that happened in my life. Now you're taking everything away from me."

"I'm sorry for everything. I'm not the right person for you. Relationships are made in heaven and we're not made for each other. It is better we forget everything and start afresh. You're every girl's dream boy. You'll find a better girl than me."

"Don't try to hide your emotions from me. Do I look like a fool to you? Don't you love me?"

"I'm not making fooling you, and no, I don't love you. We had nothing between us. I never told you that I love you. So, don't try to make a fool of yourself and leave me alone." I replied with harsh words.

"I haven't seen a liar like you. I don't want to see your face ever again," he finally said the words I wanted to listen.

"Now, you understand everything. Goodbye."

Without saying Goodbye, he started his car and went out from there. I couldn't control my tears anymore.

What did I do? I asked my soul, but I also knew that what I did was mandatory for everyone's happiness. I couldn't sacrifice everyone's happiness just for the sake of my happiness. I had so many questions for God. Why does he to do this to me always? With all that had happened, I didn't believe in God anymore.

Part-2

I reached home. Fatima aunty was sitting in the lobby. She saw me and called my name but I went straight to my room. I closed the door and closed eyes. I felt pain shoot through my heart. I didn't have any idea that we'll meet again or not. I even failed to express my love for him. I felt hopeless. Literally, I wanted to die, but I also failed in achieving that. I'm a big loser who is living life without any hope.

"Zeenat, Zeenat. Open the door!" she called.

"Fatima aunty, please leave me alone," I requested.

"Zeenat. I know you're angry with me because I didn't take your side, but I was also helpless," she said.

"I don't want to hear any explanation, please leave me alone."

"Fine. I'll go from here, but please talk to me once. If you ever thought me as your mother then please open the door."

I opened the door.

"I saw your eyes. Why were you crying?"

"I was not crying. I want to spend some time alone so please forgive me."

"What happened? Tell me!"

"I don't want to tell anything to anyone. I shared everything with you because I believed that you'll support me but I was wrong and you proved that."

"I was helpless at that time. Everyone has their own problems. You should understand this!"

"Today, I lost the person who had become the reason for my living, but I forgot about my destiny. You made me realize that I have no right to think about myself."

"You are blaming us? Seriously? We never thought anything bad about you. We love you, care for you as our daughter."

"I'm not blaming anyone. I'm blaming myself for everything. Sorry for every word, but I need some space."

"I know you had a great connection with Rajveer but you should understand the reality. He is a millionaire. His family will never accept you and you'll only cry in future."

"You're right. I agree with you, but I don't care about my future. I just wanted to live my present life with him."

"You won't understand now because you're in love. But you'll realize one day that we were right."

"Maybe, but for now please leave me alone."

"Fine. I'm going. Take care of yourself."

The days I spent with him were when I was the most contented. How could I forget those days?

The next day, I waited for him at the cafe. But then, after waiting for the whole day, I realized that he would never come. I realized that I had made a very big mistake. I wanted to contact him, but I didn't know how. Even Shanaya and Rahul didn't come to the cafe. So, I was feeling completely helpless. I had lost him.

Now, the days were like hell. One fine day, when I was doing my work in the cafe, Shanaya came and started shouting at me.

"You destroyed everything. You have played very well. But I'll never forgive you, you have to pay for this!"

"Are you mad? What are you saying?" I instantly asked.

"He tried to commit suicide. He is in the hospital and fighting for his life. You played magnificently with his feelings."

"What?"

"Yes, he is in the hospital and fighting for his life. He fell in bad company when you left him. He started drinking. Every day he fought with someone. When you came into his life, he was very happy. Slowly and gradually, he was starting to control his temper, but now you have destroyed everything. You again put him in the same condition."

"Where is he? I want to meet him, please tell me," I requested with tears.

While I and Shanaya were talking, Umar uncle came. "What happened Zeenat? Is everything alright?"

"No. Nothing is fine. Rajveer committed suicide. He took an overdose of sleeping pills. He needs me. I want to go there. I insulted him that day. I'm responsible for this. I have to go."

"Oh! Allah. Don't cry Zeenat. Everything will be fine, you go."

I went with Shanaya. I never expected this from him.

I went to his room. I saw him from the window, he was lying on the bed.

"Who are you?" a lady asked.

"My name is Zeenat."

"Oh! You're Zeenat. Are you happy now? I know your type of girls who belong to poor families. You first attract rich boys then make them fall in love with you for money, for fame and when you get everything, you leave them."

"I don't know who you are, but you have no right to blame me. I haven't done anything wrong. We were never in a relationship. I respect him for everything he did for me but please don't blame me unnecessarily for everything."

"Zeenat, she is Rajveer's mother," Shanaya said.

"Sorry, aunty. I didn't know."

"See, I don't want to hear anything. If you want to see him happy then promise me that you'll never meet him again. If you need money then I'm ready to pay anything. You just tell me what your price is?"

I was stood silently. I was unable to understand anything. They were telling me to leave him forever. They were quoting the price for my love. She was his mother. She loved him more than me. Maybe she was right, so I agreed. I agreed to leave him.

"Fine. I'll never meet him. I'll never talk to him. I don't need any money for this."

"No, you can demand anything. I'm ready to pay your price," she said.

"No, I don't need anything. Thank you. But before leaving, I just want to see him once."

"Okay, you can see. You have only three minutes."

I went to his room. He was lying on the bed. I just kissed on his forehead. I went out from there after a few minutes.

I went home and saw everyone waiting for me.

"How is he?" Umar uncle asked.

"He is fine now. He is out of danger. But today, I lost him. I want to leave."

"What happened Zeenat? Tell me everything clearly."

"Nothing. I completed your and Rajveer's parent's wish. I fulfilled everyone's wish. Don't worry. We'll never meet again."

"We never wanted this thing. We always want your good. We are not your enemies, we're your well-wishers."

"I don't know anything. I want to spend some time alone. So, please leave me and don't call me," I requested.

"Fine. We'll not disturb you. Take care of yourself."

I went to my room. I was thinking to leave the city, but whenever I thought something like this, Amma's face came in front of my eyes. She used to say, 'Always love yourself and don't let others decide your life.'

Her words always motivated me in life and showed me the right path. I decided that I will live here and just concentrate on my aim. I started living my life in my own way. Days went by fast. His birthday was next month and I promised him that I will celebrate his birthday, but I had no hope that he would come. Actually, I had lost all my hopes. I had nothing left with me. I hadn't met him for last many weeks and knew nothing about him. Life had become boring. I had stopped cursing God for everything.

Each moment of life was very difficult without him. The days somehow passed by, I was following the monotonous schedule of going home to cafe and cafe to home. That's it. Nothing interesting was happening in my life because I missed him every second. I was just resting in my room when I heard Aunty calling me."Zeenat, Zeenat. Come here."

"I'm coming," I replied.

"I know you don't want to talk to anyone. I know you have no interest in life, but I want to ask you one thing."

"Yes?"

"Does he know about your past? Does he know everything about you?"

"No, he doesn't know anything."

"Then how can you say he will accept you after knowing your past. Tell me."

"I don't know, but I trust his love. I told him that you don't know anything about my life. He told me that he doesn't care about my past. He just wants to live with me."

"Don't live life in dreams. Come out of your dreamland and be practical."

"Then what should I do?"

"Go, meet him, and just tell everything to him. If he still accepts you then I say don't leave him. He is the right person for you."

"I haven't seen him from last so many days. I don't have any idea about him. And I cannot face him now. I said so many things to him."

"Forget everything. If you want to spend your whole life with him, then you have to take this step. If he really loves you he will definitely meet you and accept you as you are."

"But Umar uncle will not allow me. I don't want to break his trust again. He did so many things for me and he is still doing."

"Don't worry about Umar uncle. I'll make him understand. You gave up your love just for us. We are not selfish. I'll do everything for you. I know I didn't take your side that day and I regret that. But today I will not step back."

"No, don't regret anything. Everyone has their own problems in life. I didn't understand and became selfish. Sorry for everything."

"Now, don't say sorry or thank you. Just concentrate on my words."

"Thank you for understanding me, motivating me, and showing me the right path in life."

"You are always welcome Zeenat," she said and hugged me.

•••

I went back to my room and felt happy because they understood me. I was really shaken up by the thought that I will meet him after so many days. I had a good feeling. I was waiting for tomorrow now.

The next day, I was working in the cafe and thinking of ways to contact him.

"Zeenat, come here," Umar uncle called me.

"Yes, sir, I'm coming."

"Sorry for that day. I realized that I was wrong."

"Please don't say sorry, you're like my father. It doesn't suit you."

"Okay. So, did you get any information about him?"

"Not yet. Nothing comes to mind. I don't know his address. I don't know anything."

"I think Ajay can help you. He knows his address. Wait, let me ask him."

"Fine, but please let me know as soon as possible."

Umar uncle called Ajay.

"Ajay, do you know Rajveer's address?"

"Yes, I think I have written it somewhere. I'll have to check."

"Then go and check. It is very important."

"Ok, sir."

He went outside and started finding his address. I prayed to God to help him. "Sir, I got it," he shouted after a few minutes,

"Sir, this is the address. But nobody knows any information about him. I think he has left the city."

"Don't assume anything. Go back to your work."

"Okay, sir."

• • •

"Zeenat, I have done my work. Now, you have to find him. Take this address."

"Yes, you're right and I'll definitely find him."

I decided that I'll go to his place tomorrow and meet him there, but Ajay's words stood like a rock in my mind. I finished my work and went home. I made masala tea and went to my room. I was taking a nap when suddenly Fatima aunty knocked the door.

"Zeenat, Zeenat."

"Yes, Fatima aunty. Why are you knocking at the door? This is your home."

"I went to the kitchen and saw someone had made masala tea, so, I came here."

"Oh! Yes, I made it. Actually, I was feeling tired and you were not there. So, I thought of making it."

"So, how was your day? Did you get any information about Rajveer?"

"It was a hectic day, but from all of these things one good thing happened, I got his house address. Tomorrow I'll go there."

"Oh! That's great. All the best!"

"Thank you very much for everything. You helped clear my confusion."

I got ready for café the next morning. After work, I would go to his house. I went to the cafe and finished my work before afternoon. I went to Umar uncle's office.

"I think I should go now," I said to Umar uncle.

"Yes, go and all the best," he instantly replied.

"Thank you for everything. Bye."

I hired an auto rickshaw from the Cafe to Lajpat Nagar.

"Bhaiya, how much time will it take to reach there?" I asked.

"Ma'am, maximum one hour."

So, I had many bad thoughts. I didn't know if I would meet him or not, his parents would allow me inside or not. But I had decided that I would not come back without meeting him. I reached Lajpat Nagar.

I asked many people the address and after walking for more than twenty-five minutes, I finally reached his home. It was a big house with a huge gate, two security guards were standing outside, they carried big sticks.

"Excuse me, Sir," I said to the security guard.

"Yes, ma'am. How can I help you?" he asked with squinted eyes.

"I want to meet Rajveer. He is my friend."

"He is not at home. You can wait for him or you can come tomorrow."

"That is ok, I will wait for him."

After waiting for two long hours I saw him. I started running towards his car.

"Rajveer, Rajveer," I shouted.

He stopped the car. "What do you want now?" he asked.

"When I was in the hospital you didn't come. You insulted me, you insulted my parents. You took money from them. You sold my love. I never asked you for anything. I just needed you. I wanted to spend my life with you, but you made fun of my love in front of everyone. I don't want to talk to you. Just go from here."

"I agree with you. I have made many mistakes, but I never insulted your parents. I didn't take a single penny from them. I was confused, but now I realize your value."

"Don't try to give me any explanations. I know everything."

"Okay, you don't want to hear me. Fine, but after three days it is your birthday and I want to celebrate it with you. So, you're coming. I will not take any excuse."

"I'm not coming."

"I trust you and I know you'll come. Your birthday is on Sunday, so Saturday night you will come to your favorite place, Benz cafe. I'll wait for you there."

"Zeenat, don't plan anything. Leave this."

"Don't make me angry. I said you're coming then it means you're coming," I said with a smile.

"Fine. I'll come."

"Thank you very much," I said and hugged him.

"I am going. I'll wait for you. I know I have hurt you. I'm responsible for everything but now I want to make everything good."

"I know you, Zeenat. You're very good by heart. I know that sometimes we are forced by situations and the same thing happened with us. So, don't worry. I will forget everything."

"Thank you for understanding me."

"My pleasure."

"Okay. It's too late. I have to leave now."

"Come, I'll drop you."

"No no. I'll go."

"I'm not asking. I'm telling you. Come fast."

He opened the doorand started his car. The way he handled the situation and heard everything was brilliant. All the way I simply looked at him, his smile moved me every time.

"Why are you sitting silently? Say something," he said.

"You are a very good human being. I don't know about our future, but whosoever will come into your life that girl will be very lucky."

"Whosoever? You are my life partner and I don't know anything else."

"We cannot decide our future. We don't know what will happen in the next second."

"You're right, but I want to spend my whole life with you, that's it."

"I think this is not the right time to think about future. Let's hope for the best."

"Ok," he smiled and stopped the car outside my house.

"Goodbye, Zeenat."

I entered and saw that Uncle-Aunty were waiting for me in the lobby area.

"What happened? Did you meet him? How's everything?"

"Everything was good. I met him. He dropped me home."

"Will he come?" uncle asked.

"Yes, he will come," I instantly replied with a smile.

"Oh! Allah, thank you very much."

"I'm very tired so I'm going to my room."

The next day while working in the cafe, I planned his birthday. I could not decide what to do, so, I decided that I should take advice from Fatima aunty. At home, after we had dinner, as she was going back to her room, I called her.

"I am so confused Aunty, I have so many ideas but unable to decide what to do. Can you give me any advice."

"Yes, sure. There are so many ways of celebrating birthdays, you just tell me how you want to do it."

"I want to celebrate it in a simple way, but he should like that."

"Okay, then you can celebrate at night. Firstly, you can cut a cake, then plan a candlelight dinner with light music. He will definitely like that."

"This is a good idea. Thank you."

Each moment looked longer as I didn't want to wait anymore. Finally, after two days, the night came. I was getting ready for his birthday.

"How am I looking?" I asked Fatima aunty.

"You're looking gorgeous."

"Thank you, I'm leaving now. Bye!"

"Bye take care!"

First, I went to the market and bought all the things for his birthday. I arrived at the cafe at 8 p.m. and started the decoration.

He came at sharp 11:56 p.m. and my happiness knew no bounds. I had switched off the lights so it was difficult for him to find his way. Exactly at 12, I switched on the lights.

"Happy birthday to you. May God bless you with opulence and gaiety!"

"Zeenat, you're looking gorgeous!"

I held his hand and took him to Umar uncle's office where I had set up the decorations.

"Wow! This is beautiful."

"Rajveer, let's cut the cake."

"Okay."

While cutting the cake, he looked at me.

"What happened Rajveer?"

"Nothing, you were supposed to say something."

"Nothing, leave it."

"Zeenat, I want to know why are you not accepting my love? Am I wrong?"

"No, it is not like that. I just don't trust my destiny because I have lost everyone who loved me. Now I don't want to lose you."

"Zeenat, we cannot predict our future on the basis of our past. Everyone has a past, the thing is we should forget everything and live in present."

"Okay. You want to listen, fine. My parents left me in an orphanage when I was just twelve. There I met Rajiya Amma who cherished me unconditionally. She loved me more than anyone else. But God took her away as well. She was murdered by the same person who raped me twice. I came here because I want to do something for the society. I want to take revenge and this is the only aim in my life. Here, I met Umar uncle and Fatima aunty, they love me like their own daughter. I'm not the right person for you, in fact, I'm not the right person for anyone. Don't spoil your life with me."

"Zeenat, I don't care about your past. I'm with you. I love your soul, not your body."

"You're very stubborn."

He held my arms and came closer. He kissed me on the forehead. Then, his lips came closer mine, they met and I got lost in his world. We started dancing on the light music that was playing and after a few minutes he went down on his knee and proposed.

"Zeenat, I love you. I want to marry you. I want to spend my whole life with you. Will you marry me?"

"Rajveer, you're very good human being and my good friend. I do have feelings for you, but I'm not sure right now. So, I need some time."

• • •

"Okay. I'll wait for your answer."

After spending some time, we came out of the cafe.

He started the bike and I sat on it. I held him tightly from behind... I wanted to live in this moment.

"Rajveer, I want to say something."

"Yes?"

"I…

Black Clouds

SUddenly a car crashed into our bike. I was crying and shouting for help but nobody came. Slowly my eyes were closed.

I don't remember exactly, but after some time I opened my eyes. I saw I waslying on the hospital bed.

"Nurse, nurse. Where am I?" I asked.

"You're in a hospital. You had an accident. you've been here for last three days," she replied.

"Where is Rajveer? He was also with me," I exclaimed.

"Rajveer! He is no more ma'am. He died two days ago."

"What? I want to see him. Where is he? I want to talk to him, he cannot leave me like this."

"Rajveer's parents took his dead body. He was cremated yesterday."

I started cursing myself. I had no words. I was crying on my destiny. Nothing was left in my life. All my hopes died.

"Why did I come to his life? Why?"

One night, as I was sleeping in the hospital, I heard some people entering my room. They were wearing masks. They tied me with a rope and injected something into my body. Slowly I fell unconscious.

The next day when I opened my eyes, I found myself lying on a bed. It was a strange place with low lighting and colorful walls.

"Don't worry. You're in the right place. Now, this is your life," a lady said.

"Who are you? I want to go to the home. Leave me."

"My name is Begum Jaan. This is my place and now you'll work for me like other girls."

"I was unable to understand any of it until the day my body was sold to someone for money. I was raped more than five times a day. The life in brothels is hell. Nobody can think or imagine it. This was my story," I said looking at Ram.

"You've faced so many things. You are a very brave woman. You're an inspiration to other girls. Seriously!"

"I don't know anything. I just have to complete my aim. I want to take revenge on everyone who destroyed my life."

"I'm with you. I'll stand by you."

"You're very good human and a friend also but I want to do this on my own. This is my fight. I hope you understand me."

"I understand everything but I can't leave you alone. You're my everything. I like the essence of your soul, not your body."

He repeated the same words which Rajveer told me. Again, love was knocking my door. This time, although my mind didn't allow me to take risk, my heart was saying that I should give him one chance.

"What happened Zeenat?"

"Nothing. I was just thinking about something."

He stood up and came towards me. His every step made me nervous. He came extremely close to me, bent one knee and said, "Zeenat, I know everything about your past. I don't care. I don't care about society. I love you and I just want to spend whole life with you."

"Ram, you're making a mistake. I'm not the right person for you and I can't think about my life again. I need time."

"I will wait for you till my last breath," he smiled as he said this.

'Love is the way of connecting two souls, not two bodies.'

To be continued...

• • •